The Neighborhood Division

Stories By

Jeff Vande Zande

WHISTLING SHADE
PRESS

Saint Paul, MN
www.whistlingshade.com

First Edition, First Printing

April 2020

ISBN 978-0-9829335-9-6

Cover illustration by Andrew Rieder

Book and cover design by Joel Van Valin

Many of these stories have been previously published in magazines and journals, including

Iron *Horse Literary Review*, *Prism Review*, *Existere*, *Fiction Circus*, *Fifth Wednesday Journal*, *Matrix*, *Coe Review*, *Jukebox Journal*, *Red Bridge Review*, The *Adirondack Review*, and *The Offbeat*.

Printed in the United States of America

Also by Jeff Vande Zande:

Detroit Muscle

American Poet

Threatened Species — A Novella and Five Stories

Landscape with Fragmented Figures

Into the Desperate Country

Emergency Stopping & Other Stories

For my wife, Jenn ... for lifting up her wings and letting me know, this must be the place.

Stories

Hearts

Refrigerator light shines into the room. Cold spills out and down and swirls around my ankles. I open the egg door and take a few, but mom's name on her bottle of medicine gets to me. It's like she's right there, watching me, and I stop. Stealing from her makes me sadder than I thought it would, sadder than it has in the past. Her with the chip diamond wedding ring and the thinning hair, her who buys these eggs just so she can stand whistling in the kitchen, making me breakfast. She always looks at me like I'm a gift. I'm not sure what I am, but I'm no gift.

Holding the bottom of my shirt, I set four eggs into the makeshift pouch. I wish I wouldn't take any, but Kurt's going to be waiting for me, and I won't be able to lie to him tomorrow. He knows my parents go to bed early. I can already hear him. "Why didn't you come back last night? What made you pussy out this time?" I close the door, and for a moment the room is completely black. Kurt was my best friend when we were kids. I'm not sure what he is now.

I'm the first to get back to the tree at the edge of the vacant lot. Danny might not make it back. His parents stay up late, and he's younger than me and Kurt.

I take the eggs out of my shirt and set them in the grass. Around me is the darkness, the near-silence, and distant squares of light I know are the windows of other houses—houses we won't egg. From where I stand, I can see the Crabshaw's house, too. Their sliding glass door glows, throwing a weak rectangle of light on the back lawn. The pane glows dimly and flickers with television light. It's the only light there. Are they watching together? Is she already in bed? Is he?

Maybe it's Mr. Crabshaw, nearly asleep—having no idea what we will soon do.

My mother sometimes tells my father that she'd like it if he'd come to bed with her instead of watching television all night. I hear more through the cold-air return than they probably would think.

Across the street, an upstairs window flickers in my house. My dad up late, in the guest room, I guess wondering if someone will call with a drywall job for him tomorrow. I hope he gets some sleep. My room is in the basement, and sometimes he comes downstairs and wakes me with his walking around late at night.

The transformers hum at the top of the telephone poles. I haven't seen a car since getting back to the tree—the tree we've gathered around since we were five or six. Then, it was enough to climb the tree. Eventually we had to see who could climb the highest, and then who could jump from the highest branch. Last year we spent twenty minutes seeing who could punch the tree the most times in a row. Most of these games were Kurt's, and he won all of them.

I look again at the Crabshaw's faint light, then my father's. I hope Kurt trips and breaks his leg on the way back here. Even as I hope it, I hear his feet shishing through the darkness towards me.

His silhouette grows darker as he fades in. He explains that it took him longer because his mom had still been awake.

"Yeah, she had a bunch of fucking questions for me," he says. "'What are you doing in the fridge?'" He mimics her with a high-pitched voice. "'I told you to eat more at supper. I told you that you'd get hungry. Make a peanut butter and jelly sandwich. Your father will want the last of the bologna...'" His voice trails off. "Bitch," he says in his own voice. He sets his eggs in the grass next to mine. "I could only get four. How many did you get?"

"Same," I say.

He nods.

I ask if he thinks Danny will make it.

"I don't know. We'll give him five more minutes."

From down the road, a set of headlights comes towards us. The light grows, flashes over us, and then disappears. Kurt studies the distancing taillights. "I think I know that guy," he says. He has some friends who can drive. Some nights they pick him up, but tonight they didn't.

Danny runs out of the darkness and almost steps on our eggs.

"Careful, dumbass," Kurt says.

"Sorry." Danny takes a few seconds to catch his breath. "Doesn't matter anyway. Look." He holds up a carton of eggs triumphantly. "Eleven," he says.

"You took all of your mom's eggs?"

He nods.

Kurt shakes his head, smiling. "Shit, that's ballsy."

Danny beams. Behind him looms the sloped darkness of the hill behind the Crabshaw's. It's a darker shadow set against the gray dark of the night. It once was the best sledding hill in the neighborhood. The Crabshaws moved in when we were in fifth grade. The hill was on their property, and they sent a letter to all the parents. Dad used the word "liability" when he tried to explain why we couldn't sled there anymore. Kurt used the word "assholes" when he heard about it.

"I have a new idea I got the other night in bed," Kurt says, "especially now that we have all these eggs from Danny."

Anymore, we can only hit the Crabshaws with five or six eggs before lights start to come on in the windows and we have to run. The shells just make too much noise. Kurt explains that we can crack the eggs into our hands and just throw the insides. "They won't hear a thing," he says, "and we can practically cover the fucking place."

A dozen and a half eggs. I can still picture Mr. Crabshaw on his ladder after the last time we got his house. We had a couple eggs each, but the Crabshaws were out of town. When they came back a few days later, Mr. Crabshaw had to use a pressure washer to get the dried egg off. Then he had to repaint. He was on a ladder for most of a Sunday.

I look again at the dark hill. "I don't know," I say, but I don't know what I'm saying.

Danny and Kurt look at me.

"What don't you know?" Kurt asks.

"Nothing."

We gather our eggs and run down through the Spatz's backyard, which butts up against the Crabshaw property. The Spatzs only have cats, so it's easy. Sometimes I wish they had dogs. Quick, barking dogs that would make this harder, maybe too hard to be worth the effort.

We crouch down behind the spruces that Mr. Crabshaw planted when he first moved in. He had no idea that we'd use them for cover. They make hitting the side of his house pretty easy. From here we can throw and run back to the tree without too much problem.

This side of their house only has three windows. Two are on the basement level, and one is on the second floor. I always guess it's their bedroom window, but I'm not sure. The lights in the room usually come on pretty quickly when we're egging.

I wish the light would come on right now.

Everything is in shadow. Kurt and Danny are just silhouettes.

"I don't think we should do this. I don't think it's right," I say. My unbroken egg is cold in my hand.

"What?" Kurt asks.

I repeat what I said.

"Right? Is it right that every time my brother tries to have a party, the Crabshaws call the cops?"

I shrug.

"And what about the hill? Is it right that they moved in and then took away the best sledding hill in the neighborhood?"

"That's a long time ago now," I say. "And my dad says they could have been sued if one of us would have gotten hurt or something."

"That doesn't matter. Why are you being a fucking pussy?"

Pussy. It's a word he's used for almost a year now.

"I'm not being a pussy."

They both stare at me—Danny right behind Kurt, like a smaller shadow of him. He changes when Kurt's around. They stood like this that night last winter, too.

"Alright, let's fight then," Kurt said. He threw down his arms and his choppers shot off his hands and into the snow, like he'd learned the move from watching hockey games.

I pushed him too far. Not far away from him Danny's smaller silhouette stood expectantly. The shadows of their frosted breath rose up and then faded. Snow mixed with night had a way of making everything silent, and Kurt's tough words hung in the air.

Tough. That's what Kurt and Danny were talking about that night last year. We were sledding on the nearby golf course. The golf course hills offered long rides, but long rides meant long walks back up the hill—sometimes in knee-deep snow. Usually we'd sled down two or three times and then stay at the bottom. We'd lie back in our sleds, look up at the sea of stars, and just talk. When we were younger, we usually talked about Christmas. But, as we'd moved up into middle school, the subjects changed to girls and toughness.

On this night we were talking about a fight that Kurt had been in a few days before. I didn't see it, but I heard that Kurt had won pretty easily. Even if I'd had the chance to see it, I probably wouldn't have. Still, I wanted to be tough or at least thought of as tough. I was actually bigger than Kurt, or at least taller.

I said that I thought I was as tough as Kurt, and when neither of them responded, I said it again. That's when Kurt challenged me to the fight.

Kurt turns around and looks at Danny. "What are you doing, dumbass? You got to crack the egg into your throwing hand."

Danny shakes his fingers, and the egg white and yolk splatter on the grass. Slick and shiny, the insides reflect the available light.

"Are you going to do this, or what?" Kurt asks, turning back to me.

I sigh. Then, I tap an egg against the trunk of the spruce and open it into my right hand. Kurt smiles. The yolk is more solid than I expect it to be. In the darkness like this it isn't yellow. No matter how I try to cup my hand, the white slips off the edges and between my fingers.

Kurt cracks an egg into his palm. We start to throw. The insides, like Kurt guessed, barely make a sound when they splash against the house. No lights come on. I only throw my four, taking my time with each one. I try to hit low, along the brick foundation where I hope it will wash off easily. Two of the eggs hit lower parts of the siding. My aim's never been very good. Kurt helps Danny empty his carton. They laugh.

Tonight, we walk back to the tree. Danny starts to say something, but stops when Kurt turns and makes one more pitch at the house. An egg, still in its shell, cracks against the single upstairs window. A light comes on a second later, and we race for the tree. Panting around the trunk, Kurt says he wanted to make things interesting.

The window stays lit for a few minutes. Even from here, about a football field away, I think I can see the shiny spots glimmering on the siding. A head appears in the window, distorted by the exploded egg and shards of shell on the glass. I feel sick. The head disappears, and a moment later the light goes out.

"That really worked," Kurt says. "If we'd have gotten more eggs, we could have covered the place."

"My mom's going to kill me," Danny says, as though he just realized that he took every egg from her refrigerator.

Kurt watches Crabshaw's. "This is fucking boring," he says after a minute. He tells us he's going to go home and call Kevin. We've never met Kevin, and only know that he is Kurt's friend with a car.

We hear the sound just before Kurt leaves. It's a ticking coming from the road. It grows louder, and we watch the edges of light thrown from a street lamp across the street. The sound is animal claws on asphalt. It appears first—a small dog, a Terrier maybe, and then its leash, and then the people walking it. The Crabshaws. They stop directly under the street light and then turn in our direction.

I don't know if they can see us or not, but I figure that they can. Their dog sniffs around the light pole. After a second, it strains at the leash. The Crabshaws don't move.

Their faces are shadowy under the light. They look sad and, without speaking, they seem to be asking us questions. Why? What have we done? Why do we deserve this? They probably don't even remember the letter about the sledding hill. Mrs. Crabshaw takes a step towards our tree, but Mr. Crabshaw touches her sleeve, and she stops.

"They've got no proof," Kurt whispers.

The three of us breathe loudly through our noses. I don't really care about proof. Behind the Crabshaws, my father's window still flickers dimly with television light.

Last New Year's Eve I couldn't sleep. My parents went to a party and left me, for the first time, without a sitter. I watched a news program that was reporting on celebrations around the world. It kept my mind off things. The confetti looked like snow.

"Did you see the ball drop?" my father asked when they finally got in around two in the morning.

I nodded.

My mother came in, wished me a Happy New Year, and then said she was going to bed.

My father stood for a moment behind me where I was sitting on the couch. He put his hand on my head. It was heavy, and his fingers made small movements in my hair. "Can't sleep?" he asked. His words seemed to move around in his mouth like marbles before they came out.

I shrugged.

He lifted his hand and then came around and sat next to me on the couch. He wrapped his arms around me and pulled me towards him. Then he kissed the back of my head. It was the first time he ever hugged me that I could remember.

"You're my boy, my son," he said. "I have love," he said. "I have so much love." He kissed my head again.

I didn't say anything.

We watched television for a few more minutes, and then I could feel his steady, sleeping breaths. His arms loosened, and I wriggled free of them. Before I went down to bed, I draped an afghan over him.

I know it was probably the alcohol he had that night, but I guess the feelings had to be there. It's the way I feel right now about the Crabshaws. Maybe this is what it's like to be drunk. Tears well up in my eyes.

They look at each other and then Mr. Crabshaw gives the leash a little tug. The dog strains again to keep walking, but then follows its owners back in the direction they came. They step out of the light and disappear.

"What was that about?" Danny whispers.

Kurt starts to laugh, half genuine and half forced. His laughter grows louder, and then crescendos until they must be able to hear him.

Last winter, when Kurt told me to fight him, I didn't. I was afraid.

"You said you were as tough as me," he said. "Prove it. Let's fight."

I could tell he didn't really want to beat me up, but he couldn't let me go on as I had been either. Toughness needed to be earned.

"Okay," I finally said, "You're tougher. But, I'm smarter." I wanted to be something. And, it was true. I was smarter. I was in harder classes. I'd tested into the Hearts, and Kurt was only a Club. The teachers didn't tell us what the cards meant—Diamonds, Spades—but it wasn't hard to figure out that the Clubs were the kids who struggled in school. They were also usually the toughest kids.

Kurt shrugged. "Okay," he agreed. "You're smarter." He gave it to me quickly, like I had claimed that I was the best at sewing or setting a table.

I'm not a fighter, but I run at Kurt, fists swinging. I don't land one on him anywhere he's going to feel it. When he figures out what I'm doing, he jabs one punch in my stomach, and I'm down.

"What the hell are you doing?" he asks.

I look up and catch a sobbing breath. I'm crying, but it's from more than just the pain in my gut. "I think you're an asshole," I manage to get out.

It's quiet except for my sobs. Kurt studies me and then shakes his head. "Crybaby pussy," he says. He walks away. Danny follows.

I lie for a moment in the grass until my stomach doesn't hurt as much. I can still imagine the Crabshaws standing under the streetlight. They look so alone surrounded by all that night. I close my eyes and try to shake away the image of them.

I'm not even all that smart. That would at least be something. Everyone knows the Diamonds are the smartest kids. I don't know what I am. Maybe I'm just a pussy, like Kurt always says.

Smoulder

Mrs. Sewell haunted my thoughts for almost three months. Now, one hand on the doorknob and the other gripping the doorframe, she looks haunted herself. Poltergeist. Demons. I don't know what, but she doesn't look good—like she's been alone in a dark place for too long. Mainly it's her eyes. Puffy. Bloodshot. Dark circles. She studies my face like she doesn't even know me. "Come in," she says after some silence.

She tells me not to bother, but I take my shoes off in the foyer. They're covered in old paint—look like one of those Pollack paintings. I'm trying to pretend that I'm here because she has another painting job for me, but I think I know why she called. She leans her weight against the wall. She's wearing a white turtleneck. Whatever the last year has done to her eyes, it sure hasn't touched her body. She's wearing a skirt, too, and her legs ... wow.

Guilt hits me for thinking this way. I remember my talk with Mr. Sewell on my father's porch almost a year ago.

He sat on the porch swing staring down, rocking slowly.

"She told me everything," he said, looking up when I stepped out through the screen door. The whites of his eyes were pink.

My dad suggested I try to get more money out of him, tell him I underestimated the job. I was just hoping to get off the porch with my life.

The way Mr. Sewell stared into my eyes, fists clenched, I was ready for anything. My dad was in the house, and I imagined myself yelling for him, just so I'd be able to do it if I really needed to.

"She's sick," Mr. Sewell said. He stood up. "Depressed. On pills. Do you like taking advantage of people?"

I couldn't say anything. I just stood there, waiting.

"I was never going to leave her," he said. "She wanted to give me an excuse. You were an excuse. Nothing more. She hates herself. She's all burned up. Gone."

I waited.

He unclenched his fists. "You can consider yourself paid," he said. He stepped down the stairs and then stopped on the sidewalk. "She's dead inside."

"I don't think so," I managed, watching Mr. Sewell pull away.

"I saw your card in the grocery store," Mrs. Sewell says, slipping slightly on the wall and then catching herself.

"I get some business that way," I say. She's really drunk, but I can't leave. I'm not fooling myself. I know why I'm here.

"I..." She stops, smiles slightly. "We were your first, though, right? Your first ... job?" Her eyes are glossy.

I nod. "Gotten better since then. Even have a couple guys on my crew now."

"You never forget your first job," she says.

I look down. I can feel the heat in my cheeks. "No, you don't."

When I first came to the Sewell's, I was still living in my father's house. I couldn't paint to save my life.

Dad rapped on my door and then opened it. "Finish that job, yet?" he asked. His acne scars gave his skin a ruddy, pocked appearance.

I shook my head.

"No? How many jobs you going to get at this rate?"

I shrugged.

"You're over there ten hours a day! What they want in that neighborhood, the Sistine Chapel?"

"It's a big house. I'm taking my time. I want to do it right and get some recommendations." Dad was always after me about getting a job after Mom died.

He crossed his arms. "What are you charging for this masterpiece?"

"Three hundred."

He said the price back at me. "Gerry, you borrowed seven hundred from me to get your equipment."

"I know."

He shook his head for a long time. "What's that doing in here?" he asked, pointing to the mini-refrigerator humming next to my bed.

I looked at the fridge. "It was in the basement. I just brought it up to keep some pop in here."

He started shaking his head again. He sighed. "Television, refrigerator, dvd player ... this isn't an apartment. It's a bedroom. Your bedroom since you were a kid. I mean, don't you think you oughta think about moving out sometime? I was married at your age."

I sniffed and looked out my window.

He took a step forward. "I didn't mean ... I know it's hard. I know. I got lucky with Mom. I always said that. You'll come around. You ... you'll be fine. Just fine."

I sniffed again.

"You're a handsome guy. I see it."

"Dad..."

"You always have this room. Never mind what I said."

When he left, I tried to finish the sitcom I was watching before he came in, but I couldn't find anything funny in it. I hurled the remote control at the screen.

I follow Mrs. Sewell down a long, cream-colored hallway. The paintjob is mine. It could be better—I see that now. But still, it's not bad. She sets her hand against the wall.

"I didn't think you'd come right today," she says without turning to look at me.

"I was in the neighborhood," I say, knowing I was over fifteen miles away.

In the living room, she falls more than sits on the couch. Straightening up, she smoothes her skirt and takes a pack of cigarettes and a lighter from the coffee table. We're in the first room where I really learned how to paint. I'll never forget this room. My heart's really going.

She lights a cigarette and blows smoke over her head. "You look different," she says. "I can't... I..."

"Dermatologist," I say. "I'm finally on decent health coverage."

She nods. "You must have girls now."

I shrug. "I guess." I've been on a few dates that my guys have set me up on. I really don't know what to do. Sometimes I think they want me to do something, but I'm all locked. If you think of yourself one way for a long time, you just think of yourself that way. It's hard to think of yourself as a person someone might want.

She leans back and then forward, like she's trying to keep me in focus. "Do you need a drink?"

I should leave. She's so drunk. I keep remembering what Mr. Sewell said about her being sick. I keep looking at her legs, too.

I ask her if she has beer. "Be right back," she says. Launching herself to standing, she staggers to the door that leads to the kitchen. It still doesn't quite swing closed. It's the door I heard them through when she and Mr. Sewell were arguing. I watched them through the crack.

"On the train ... in the dining car," she said, lighting a cigarette. "His hand was on my leg, and I pushed it off." She took a drag. "After we went through a tunnel, his hand was on my leg again, and I left it there."

Mr. Sewell cleared his throat. "I don't get... It wasn't okay and then it was?"

She said that it was something like that. She tapped her cigarette into the ashtray too many times. The cherry snapped off and smoldered among the butts.

Mr. Sewell dug his thumb nail into the table.

"Allen? Do you really think anything more could have happened? Do you think anyone ... that desperate?" She took a long drag. "It just felt nice for awhile. Leave it at that, okay?"

Stirring my paints, the idea of some guy's hand on Mrs. Sewell's thigh drove me crazy. I fantasized that it was my hand—the feel of her flesh under my palm. I thought about it at night in my father's house. I squeezed my own thigh just to have some idea. Then, I got out of bed and locked my door. I slept soundly afterwards.

Mrs. Sewell had been making noise in the kitchen, but I don't hear it anymore. Maybe she went up to the bedroom and passed out. This is my chance, but I can't get my legs to work. I gotta see where this might go, where I hope it's going. Ten hours could pass, I'd still be sitting here.

When I was in this room last, it was covered in drop cloths. I look at the kitchen door, waiting for her to come through it. I remember the last time she did.

Mr. Sewell hired me because I was cheap. He didn't know that I'd never painted before. The cut line at the top of the wall wavered, dotting and dabbing yellow onto the white ceiling. I found white paint in the basement and tried to touch up the mess.

Mrs. Sewell walked into the room. "Now you're getting white on the yellow."

I stepped down the ladder a few rungs. She was right. I looked at her. "I'll touch that up later. I think I'm getting better."

The front door opened and then slammed.

She looked in the direction of the sound. She looked back at me. "He wants me to fire you."

"What? Why?"

She exhaled, lowering herself slowly onto the couch. She made a pained face and adjusted her torso. "You're not very good."

I reminded her how little I was charging.

"It looks terrible at any price," she said. "His words, not mine."

I stepped off of the ladder. "I guess I'll pack up my equipment," I said. I couldn't imagine what my father would say.

She took a drag, exhaled, and then smiled. "I said he wanted me to fire you. I didn't say I was going to. I like having you in the house." She rubbed her cigarette into an ashtray. "Take a break. Sit down for a minute."

I sat in a chair.

She leaned back into the couch cushions. "Would you believe I used to be a model?"

I looked at her. "You could be a model now."

She smiled the first smile I'd seen on her face that wasn't tinged with sadness. "Thank you." She reached for her smokes. "That's how Mr. Sewell and I met. He was just a young photographer then."

I nodded.

"Then, we were in love, like everyone starts out, I suppose. There was an accident, though. What happened you usually think only happens to other people. But now we're other people. Anymore he almost always finds a reason to go into the city on business." She took a quick puff. "Like now. He won't be home until Sunday."

I swallowed and nodded again.

She patted a cushion. "Sit next to me."

I stood and switched over to the couch. My heart banged against my ribs like it was in a paint shaker. I felt I knew what she might do, what she might let happen—like that hand on her leg—but then I also knew that nobody would want that with me.

She smoked the rest of her cigarette. "You've never had a girlfriend, have you?"

It was like a switch. I felt the tears coming up. I shook my head.

"Never had a girl touch you."

I ran a sleeve across my eyes.

"It's okay," she said. She put her hands on my face and ran her finger tips lightly over my cheeks, forehead, and chin. Sliding under her touch, my blemishes, acne, and cysts were made plain to me, like looking in a mirror. I felt her feeling my ugliness.

"Skin can be so cruel," she said.

Her breath was hot with liquor when she leaned in and kissed me. I never felt anything like it. Warm, wet, giving. I disappeared in it, not aware of paint or my father or my own ravaged face. I existed, for the moment, only in this new, kind darkness. It was a vortex pulling me joyously into her hot mouth. We kissed for a long time, and then I reached and found her soft breasts.

Her grip on my wrists was strong. I opened my eyes. Tears were streaming from hers.

"I'm sorry," I gasped. "I didn't... I just..."

Shaking her head, she quieted me. Still holding my wrists, she spread my arms over the back of the couch. "Keep them there. If you touch me, I'll stop."

I nodded. I would have agreed to anything, only wanting her to kiss me again.

She lowered her head into my lap. My zipper. Her hands. A moment later, my own hands closed tightly around the drop cloth under my palms.

Afterwards, she lay for a moment with her head on my thighs. I wanted to run my fingers through her hair, but didn't dare risk it. She breathed deeply. "The white paint you're using to touch up the ceiling," she said, rising up and to her feet. "It doesn't match the original."

She walked out through the kitchen door.

I open my eyes. Something suddenly comes to me, something I'm putting together just now.

Mrs. Sewell pushes open the door from the kitchen. She's holding a beer. "We had some down in the basement," she says. Her hair is matted on one side. She runs her hand through it, fluffs it out. "There's a couch down there, too. I had a quick little cat nap." She laughs. Handing me the beer, she sits down next to me.

I smile. "Aren't you drinking?"

"I've had enough," she says.

I take a drink. The beer's warm. "I was just thinking," I start, "about the last time we were in this room together."

"Oh?"

"Afterwards, I mean. I came back that next Monday, but you weren't around at all. I checked the whole house."

She lights a cigarette. "It wasn't you," she says. "I was just ... the night before..."

"No. I mean, I wasn't ... it's just that I remember that day, that week." I tell her about how I found my brushes stiff with yellow paint. After what she'd done, I didn't have a mind left to remember to clean up. "I didn't have money for new brushes. I waited for you until noon or so, and then I left." I tell her I wasn't sure why, but I stopped by the library and checked out a book on painting. "I think because of you," I say. "I wanted to give ... I wanted to give you something. I didn't have much ... it's just that I figured I could paint this room right for you."

She exhales, looking around. "It does look good."

"Because of you," I say.

She smiles.

"I went home that night and like the book said, I heated up vinegar and soaked my brushes. I combed them through in the morning with an old fork. They were like new. I read other things in the book. I read about cutting in. I just read and read." I tell her about that week, how I had her house to myself, and I just redid the whole thing. "There were times that I wasn't even thinking about you ... that just the painting and getting it right became something important."

She frowns a little and mashes out her cigarette.

"No, it's not that ... I mean, it was always about you ... for you. It's just that on that Friday, when I was pulling drop cloths off the furniture, packing up my equipment ... it's just something, I don't know. I'd become a painter. I was good at something."

She drops her hot hand on my leg. "You were a good kisser. I didn't tell you that, but you were." She leans forward and keeps leaning.

"I really think I should go," I say.

"Don't," she says, still leaning.

I lean back into the arm of the couch, letting her lie on top of me. Closing my eyes, I'm in that dark world again—dark with pleasure and everything animal. Her mouth on mine. I could live here. But there's something else in this world now, too. It's nagging, telling me I should stop this, that it isn't right. She's sick. On pills. I'm here to take something. The way she gives it, it almost feels like I'm stealing.

She tells me to put my hands up over my head. We kiss again. I imagine what she's going to do and, risking everything, I sweep my left hand down along the floor, come up, and squeeze her right breast. It's soft in my hand for a moment and then disappears.

Wincing, she wrenches herself up and off of me.

Something hot burns up my spine. "What ... what happened ... did ... did I hurt you?"

She turns her back to me, groping violently up through the bottom of her turtleneck. She repeats the words "damn it" over and over. Her elbows jut awkwardly from her sides. After a moment, she pitches something across the room violently. It lands almost without a sound behind a chair. She collapses into the couch, sobbing.

I touch her shoulder and then draw my hand away. "What ... are you? What?"

"Just leave."

I sit frozen. I want to cry myself. I have no idea. "What ... I don't ... I don't understand."

"Leave!"

I tell her I don't understand what I did.

"You didn't do ... just, please. Just please leave." Her words are broken up with sobbing.

I stand slowly. I sit down again. Something tingly rushes over me, but it's not good, like the feeling you get just before throwing up. "I can't. I can't just leave. I can't..."

"I'm asking you," she says, her voice less shaken with sobs. "I'm asking you to please just go."

"And I'm saying I can't."

She doesn't say anything else. We sit this way for awhile. Looking around, I study the room, the paint. I'm not sure what to do. Her back convulses now and again with the quick breaths that follow crying. She stays turned from me, hugging one of the pillows. She talks into it. "Why are you still here?"

"I'm not going to leave. I'm going to stay until..."

"Until what?" she turns toward me. "Until you know. Until you..."

Something is wrong. Her chest. Her right breast is gone.

She sees where I'm looking. "Is this what you have to know?" She grabs the bottom of her turtle neck and pulls it up to her chin. I blink. I go numb. Her torso is a patchwork of pink, white, brown, red, and black. Pieces of her look ready to flake off. It's like what's left under wallpaper when you tear it away—patches of glue, backing, chunks torn from the drywall surface. The right cup of her bra sits deflated, empty. The left cup has no breast either. It's filled with some kind of soft, flesh-tone plastic. The burns go down below her waistline.

She pulls the turtleneck back down over herself. Tears streak her cheeks. "We both know why you're here," she says. "You don't have to stay."

"I'm here because you called me," I say.

"Yes, I called you. And now I'm asking you to leave."

I swallow. I don't get up. I touch my fingers against each other, but barely feel it.

She starts to talk. She says it happened fifteen years ago. "We were all on a beach somewhere near the Hamptons." She says some hotshot editor at a big magazine was having a party. "It was night," she says. She says she was drunk. "The others decided to go skinny dipping. I didn't go, but then I thought of Allen out there with the other models, naked. I just ... I got up." She says when she stood, she passed out. "Allen said I fell right onto the fire. I was on it for awhile before any of them could make it to shore and drag me off."

She's different to me now. Sad. It happens that quickly.

"Just go now," she says. "Just stop looking at me like that. I won't blame you for going. Just go."

I stand up. "I don't really ... I mean, why did you call me? Why when you found my card in the grocery ... why even that first time."

She turns her back to me. "Just never mind. Just go."

"I'm just asking why you called me."

She sighs. "It doesn't just go away," she says a few seconds later.

"What?"

"Whatever I am, whatever I feel, it's not this. It's not this shell of a body. The want. The need to feel and to want to make someone ... when I was with you the first time, it was to get Mr. Sewell to ... but then I felt something else, too. I was still alive under all of this. Being able to ... I just didn't think I could feel that way. And making someone else feel that way..." She buries her face in her hands. "Don't make me talk about it anymore. Just go."

What she says, it's everything I felt—sometimes still feel. It's why I'm here now. She made me feel like maybe ... I don't know. She gave me something, something more than what she gave me. I sit down and turn her towards me. I gather her into my arms.

"Don't," she says. She sobs into my shoulder.

I hold her tightly. I caress her back.

"I've been so alone," she says. "Everyone's sorrow, their pity, your pity now ... it does nothing. Allen stayed with me out of pity. It killed both of us."

I hold her. When I don't hear her crying anymore, I put my hand under her chin. I lift her lips to mine.

"You shouldn't," she says. "You can't."

I kiss her. I'm not sure how long. I can feel her in the dark world with me. I reach my hand up and under the turtleneck. Her skin feels like a stucco wall. I imagine what my face felt like under her fingers.

She pulls back from the kiss and looks down. "I don't feel anything," she says. "I don't. The nerves. It's all dead."

I slide my hand into her skirt feeling for where the burns end—if they end.

She pulls back from my kiss and shakes her head. "Nothing," she says.

I look at her.

"Please don't stop," she says.

The Long Run

The man caressed an electric razor around his squared jaw, looking as though he'd found his calling. Then, a woman slipped into the bathroom behind him and smoothed her palm over his cheeks. "I love to get my hands on an Epic man," she told the camera.

Andy touched one of the buttons under his fingers. The screen went black.

Brenda looked at him. "What are you doing?"

"I can't stand it anymore," he said, gesturing toward the television. "These commercials are so fu ... they're insulting. I feel like some kind of idiot sitting here. I mean, I think I could take it if they'd just show a picture of the damn thing and talk about how good it shaves, but they have to have that asshole in the bathroom like he's really shaving and—"

"Who are you?"

He looked at her. She was playful, smiling. "I don't know," he said. "Sorry."

She studied him. "Well, whoever you are, could you turn the TV back on? I was watching that."

He touched the button again. Gregory Peck took aim on a rabid dog in the distance. Andy thrust himself up from the couch and walked over to the window. It was early April. The overnight snow had dusted their lawn. More was coming down. Branches of the surrounding pines shimmied and swayed in the intermittent gusts. Andy recalled going down to the box for the newspaper earlier that morning. Bewildered robins hopped around the backyard. What was this cold place they had migrated home to?

"I think I'm going to go for a run," Andy said.

Atticus pulled the trigger, and the dog yelped its death. "Didn't you know your daddy is the best shot in this county?"

"Oh hush, Hec," Atticus said, "Let's get back to town."

"You're going to what?" Brenda said.

"I've got to do something. It doesn't feel like I've done anything."

"I thought your dad was coming this afternoon to watch the game."

He turned from the window. She was still watching the movie while she talked. "I'll be back in plenty of time," he said. "I'm just going to go downtown and back—just a few miles."

She told him he could unpack the rest of the boxes in the basement if he wanted something to do.

"I will sometime this week. I just want to get a run in."

She looked at him. "Oh ... Kay," she sang.

He rummaged through a few boxes in one of the spare rooms before he found sweat pants, a sweat shirt, and an old pair of running shoes. Unbuttoning his shirt, he looked at his pale gut and the shadowy ravine folded around his navel when he sat. He needed to workout more than once or twice a week. Even three times a week was just maintenance. He wasn't even sure what he got out of the elliptical machine, anyway. It always felt so easy, comfortable.

He pulled a second pair of sweat pants over the first and went to the basement to find a hat and gloves. Zipping a windbreaker over the sweatshirt, he told Brenda that he would be back within a half hour.

"Have fun," she said.

A sharp wind hit him as he turned out of his cul-de-sac onto Juniper Dr. He didn't even seem to feel it. The cold felt good more than anything. Passing several driveways, he nodded his head at his idea for taking a run. His legs and lungs felt ready for some distance. He followed Juniper Dr. to Pine Bluff Blvd. and that to Alpine Terrace Dr. Going out through the gatehouse and onto the sidewalks of the main street, he checked his watch. He'd been running for six minutes. What kind of time was he making? He felt like he was going at a good clip.

He had hoped that the new position would mean something. Turned out that a regional manager wasn't very different from a district manager. The politics were the same. His days were the same. His house was bigger.

They were closer to his parents, too. He wasn't sure if that was a benefit or drawback. He looked at his watch again. Ten minutes. He'd already gone at least a mile. Farther, he thought. His legs felt as though he could run all day.

He looked up briefly into the windshield of a rusty pickup truck. The teenager in the passenger seat flipped him the bird. Andy looked away.

An eighth of a mile ahead, the two and three-story buildings of the downtown faded into each other for a four-block stretch. Bistros. Boutiques. A Starbucks. It was this bedroom community's excuse for a downtown, something like a shopping mall. It was nothing like the cacophonous downtowns of his youth. Dayton, Cincinnati, Detroit—the places his father had moved the family as he'd chased his fortune. He'd finally retired from a mid-level management position at GM when the pensions were still fat. He spent his free time gardening when his back didn't hurt too much. It was a hobby that had surprised even Andy's mother.

In the distance, people were shopping. Going into stores. Coming out. Another jogger, a black shape moving faster than the others, turned off the main street between two stores. Probably headed for the groomed running path that ran alongside the Grand River.

Crossing Third St, Andy looked to his right. Could he follow Third and find some back way into his neighborhood, some kind of route that would loop him around?

Reaching the other side of the street, he turned right, away from the downtown. He wanted more than just going downtown and back. He liked the idea of finding some new path home. The wind was against his back, pushing him along.

Still, he didn't know where he was going. He checked his watch again. Thirteen minutes. If he turned around, he'd have time to shower and get some snacks ready for the game.

He kept running.

A block ahead, an old man turned out of a driveway toward him, moving meticulously behind a walking stick. Andy stopped a few feet in front of him.

"Do you know where this road goes?" he asked, pointing.

The old man turned and looked down the street. "Well—"

"I'm just wondering if there's a back way into the Alpine neighborhood."

The man turned back toward Andy. He put both hands on his stick and leaned. "Which Alpine?"

"Terrace."

He looked thoughtful. "I'm not sure where that one—"

The sweat on Andy's upper lip began to cool. "It's where the old boy scout camp used to be."

The old man smiled. "Okay. I know where you mean, now. I was a part of that camp when I was a kid." His forehead furrowed. "There's a back way, but you gotta know your way around. Better off just sticking to—"

Andy told him that he wanted to make a circle so he didn't have to backtrack. "You said there's a way?"

"There's a way." He turned again and pointed into the distance. "Just stay on Third. It's going to twist you through some neighborhoods, but you'll come out on Lee. Take a right on Lee and go past East Ridge. When you come to West Ridge, turn in there and follow it around to Maltby. Take Maltby to Hamburg and that should get you there, but—"

"Lee to West Ridge, West Ridge to Maltby and Maltby to Hamburg," Andy recited.

The old man nodded, dabbing his fingertips at the snow in his eyebrows. "What do you think of our April weather?"

Andy launched back into his run. "It's not too bad," he called back over his shoulder.

He guessed that the houses along Third represented the older part of the town—what it used to be before all of the Alpine Terraces, Vistas, Ridges, and Views began to spring up. The homes around him were small, neat, and not separated by acres of lawn. A few men were on a roof pitching shingles into a dumpster in the driveway. A plastic Santa Claus was still tied to the chimney.

Andy's sweat held a skin of warmth around him. The cold and snow in the air did nothing. Starting to climb a hill at the end of Third, he checked his watch. Twenty minutes. His thighs burned against the hill's incline. He clapped his hands a few times, encouraging himself. "Come on," he whispered, smiling.

Just past the crest of the hill the road came to a T intersection. Must be Lee, he thought, but the sign had too many letters. The words came into focus. Meadow Valley Lane.

Andy stopped and caught his breath. Meadow Valley Lane curved to the right on his left and curved to the left on his right. It was flanked in both directions by newer builds that had probably gone up within the last five years.

Where was Lee? Andy shivered. He'd stood still too long. Turning to the right, he started running again.

Meadow Valley crossed Meadow Ridge, Meadow Downs, and Meadow Forest—each one a cul-de-sac. The next, Meadow Creek, wasn't a dead end, and Andy turned left onto it, hoping that an end to the cul-de-sacs meant the neighborhood would soon spill him out onto Lee. He adjusted his slipping hat. The insides of his gloves were soggy and warm. After a minute, Meadow Creek met up with Meadow Valley again. Andy turned right toward a cross-street in the distance. Maybe it was Lee. Sweat dripped out of his hair and down his back.

The street, when he came to it, was Meadow Valley—the same Meadow Valley he'd turned off of to come down Meadow Creek. Meadow Valley was just a big circle. His thoughts went to the idea of turning around. Then, the hrmmm of faster-moving traffic pulled his attention south. A busier road. He turned left off of Meadow Valley onto Meadow Valley and followed the sound.

Andy crested a rise. Another T intersection ahead. The cars on the new road were moving at least fifty miles an hour. He felt a surge, something nearly electric moving through him. The street sign. Just a few letters. Just a couple. It's short. Just a ... Lee. It was Lee. "Yes," he whispered.

Coming to the end of Meadow Valley, he could hear the old man's voice. Right onto Lee. Andy had made it. He looked into the passing cars, suddenly wanting to make some kind of contact, share his small victory. The drivers were just blurs behind the wheel. They didn't care that Andy had reached Lee.

Go past East Ridge, he remembered. He checked his watch. He'd been running for twenty-eight minutes. His ankles ached. A dull pain haunted his right knee, the ghost of an old injury from his early twenties, before he'd met Brenda, before the job, when he used to run ten miles every other day.

Lee was an old county road with no shoulder for running and no houses. Just a few trailer homes at the end of long dirt driveways. When he heard cars behind him, he moved into the overgrown edges, almost twisting his ankle on the uneven ground. He stayed on the asphalt as much as he could, but the cars kept coming, and the drivers came close on his left, as though they hadn't seen him, as though they were startled to find him suddenly there—a dark shape trudging through the sleet. Had Brenda noticed how long he'd been gone? He hoped that Maltby was closer than Lee had been, and maybe Hamburg would be closer still. A forty minute run would be good. He was ready to be done.

In the near distance, he made out a large stone marker with the name of a neighborhood etched into its flat surface. He ran closer. East Ridge. Not more than an eighth of a mile later he found the entrance to West Ridge on the other side of the road. Everything was coming together. He waited out a few cars and then cut across the street and into the recently-developed neighborhood. Lee past East Ridge, West Ridge to Maltby, Maltby to Hamburg and Hamburg home. He repeated it in his head as West Ridge Boulevard took him past cross street after cross street, none of which were Maltby.

His shoulders were sore where his arms had rocked back and forth in the joints. His lower back and feet ached. His pace had slowed to nearly twelve-minute miles. He looked around for someone he might ask about Maltby. Though cars and SUVs were parked in every driveway, no person ever seemed to be outside.

He had been running for nearly forty-four minutes when the busier street at the T intersection ahead of him finally turned out to be Maltby.

What direction had the old man said? Andy looked left. Driveways. A few houses. They looked familiar enough that they might have been houses on the outskirts of his neighborhood. He scanned ahead for any sign of Hamburg. He started running again.

Run faster. Run faster. Maltby was hilly, and his body couldn't give him anymore. At the crest of each hill, he squinted ahead through the falling snow. No cross streets. He'd been running for nearly an hour by the time he'd crested the fourth hill. A sign welcomed him to Shelby Township. A sign further up the road on the left read, Scanton Middle School. He'd never heard of the township or the school. Farther from home, he felt the edges of panic. The details of a new plan came into his head as though they were being spoken to him.

Turn around. Backtrack. He'd keep an eye out for people in driveways so he could borrow a cell phone. Brenda had to be worried. Maybe his father was already there. Andy could hear him: "Be nice if I at least had a grandchild to watch the game with me since my son can't bother to show up." If the old man started to worry, he'd drive up and down every street in the city. He had to let them know that he was fine. Keep running. If he walked, it would be at least another two hours before he'd get home.

He turned around. After a moment, he passed the entrance to the middle school again. The familiarity of it filled his body with a heaviness. Stopping at the sound of a car coming behind him, he spun and stuck his thumb in the air. The driver stared blankly ahead. A few more cars came. A pickup. Each passed as though he weren't even there. No slowing. No glances. Not even a middle finger. Looking down, he saw the sweat that had soaked through his layers. He looked as though he'd had an accident with incontinence. Nobody was going to stop. Nobody was going to help him get home. It was his quest alone, a result of his own foolishness.

When he tried again, he couldn't will himself into anything faster than a walk. He dragged his feet along the gravel. His sweat began to cool, making him shiver. What the hell had he done? Why didn't he just run downtown and back?

He was an idiot.

Then, in the grass just beyond the shoulder, he saw it. A sign. Fallen and lying on the snowy ground. It was a metal real estate sign for Alpine Terrace. *New Models. Luxurious Living. Must See.* The arrow pointed straight ahead.

His heart and mind raced.

That was it. He had turned left on Maltby when he should have turned right. To the right, Maltby hooked up with Hamburg. It had to. That's why the arrow pointed straight ahead. Alpine Terrace. He wasn't far from home. He pushed himself back into a limping run. He had to land his right foot at an odd angle to keep his knee from registering a sharp twinge.

That's all it was. He'd taken one wrong turn. He passed the entrance to West Ridge. There'd be no backtracking. Hamburg had to be ahead. He nodded to himself when he saw a road sign warning that there was a stop coming up. The stop sign would be where Maltby met Hamburg. It will be Hamburg, he thought.

He came to the stop sign. Hamburg Road, as he'd guessed. To his left another road met up with Hamburg on its opposite side. He read the sign. Hamburg Road. What the hell! Two Hamburg Roads?

He had three choices. Left, right, or down the other Hamburg. Each could take him in the wrong direction. He checked the shoulders for another real estate sign, another arrow.

Nothing.

"Sonuvabitch," he said. Then he yelled it. Across the street there were woods, framed on either side by one of the Hamburg Roads. He stared into the trees in disbelief. He was going to have to backtrack. There was no other choice. Maltby back to West Ridge back to Lee back through the Meadow neighborhoods back to Third back to main back to Alpine Terrace Dr. At the least, two hours.

Gazing into them, something about the woods came to him. Something. Something odd, different. Something ... light. The trees, instead of fading into deeper blackness, seemed to open out of the darkness in the distance. A meadow? A lake? Maybe his neighborhood? It didn't make any sense. Still, he couldn't deny the urge he had to cut through the woods—to just see where they might go. A part of his mind kept telling him that he would only get more lost—the kind of lost that backtracking wouldn't undo, the kind of lost that calls for search parties.

Ignoring that part of his mind, he crossed the street and pushed his way through the brush into the woods. If the trees thinned in the distance, they made up for it in their thickness all around him. He couldn't run. Branches scraped along his cheeks and pulled his hat from his head. He left it and pressed on for several more minutes.

It was a mistake. The woods weren't thinning. It was a trick of the light—light playing off the snow-covered forest floor. He was going to get lost.

Pushing ahead, trying to run again, wanting so badly to come out into some kind of clearing, he caught a foot against a fallen birch and hit the ground, knocking the wind out of himself.

After a moment he could breathe again. He rolled over and stared into the branches above him. Each was freckled with green buds. The sweat soaked through his clothes that had been keeping him warm, loose, now soaked up the ground's cold, chilling him. His tracks through the woods would still be fresh. He could find his way back to the road. Find a house. Knock on a door. Call home and end this.

No, resounded in his head. He calmed himself with deep breaths and checked his watch. He'd only been in the woods for seven minutes. He had to keep going. This was his path to make. No more roads. No more wrong turns or backtracking. The snow came down through the branches and landed on his face. It was April, and it was snowing. Feeling a way he hadn't felt before, he crouched and then stood.

Holding up his arm, he followed it, blazing a way through the myriad of branches. He stepped over fallen trees. This has to lead somewhere, he thought. Coming out on the other side, he would have to be closer to home, closer to some place. The woods would have to end. His heart raged against his ribs, not from his pace or fear, but from something he couldn't name.

The trees did finally begin to thin. He could make out bricks ahead of him. A sliding glass door. He came out of the woods and into someone's backyard. He was in a neighborhood. He'd come through the woods.

He laughed.

The silhouette of a head in a window seemed to notice him. He sprinted through the yard along the side of the house and down to the curb. Huge houses loomed around him. He ran to the end of the street and checked the sign. Alpine Terrace Ct.

He'd made it.

Jesus Christ, he thought, filled with himself, smiling. He ran along the streets, recognizing each as it brought him closer to his house.

His father's car was in the driveway. At least he wasn't out looking for him. Andy had been gone for an hour and forty-five minutes when he finally opened the door.

He stood for a moment in the foyer untying his shoes slowly. He couldn't place what he was feeling, standing in the entrance to this home he barely knew.

"Is that you, Andy?" Brenda called from the kitchen. "Where have you been?"

Leaning against the wall, he let a shoe drop to the floor. "I don't really know."

"What?"

"Get in here, boy. Look at this," his father said, chuckling.

Andy walked into the living room. His father was reclined in the leather La-Z-Boy. He looked older than the last time Andy had seen him.

"Tigers are playing, and she has me watching this." He pointed at the television.

"Oh for God's sake, they're losing four to nothing," Brenda said. "You've had plenty of chances to change the channel."

Andy looked at the screen.

"The summer that had begun so long ago had ended," Scout narrated, "and another summer had taken its place. And a fall."

"So where have you been?"

Andy looked back to his father. "Just out running. I was trying to find another way into the neighborhood. I got turned around on some back roads."

Brenda came in from the kitchen and set a tray of chicken fingers and ranch dressing on the table. "I told you it would be something like that," she said. She looked at the television and then back at Andy's father. "There. It's over. Are you happy? Now you can go back to watching the Tigers lose."

"It was bizarre," Andy started. "I was out there—"

"Lose? The Tigers love to play behind the eight ball. They play their best when they're coming from behind."

Andy absently bent for a chicken finger, waiting for his chance to try to explain.

"Oh, God, don't eat. Go take a shower. You're disgusting, Andy."

He nodded, leaving the room.

"Hurry up," Brenda said. "You don't want to miss the Tigers' next error."

"You just be quiet," his father said.

Andy stood in the bathroom pulling his wet clothes from his weary body. He dropped them in a pile until he was naked and then shivered off a chill. How far had he gone? Nine miles? Ten? He'd been lost. The snow had drifted down past the green buds to his face as he lay on the ground. He came through the woods. He trusted something, and the only name he could give it was instinct. Afterwards, his heart felt like an animal rabid in his rib cage.

Then it was over.

He'd learned the roads, the turns. He knew the way to get there again. And still, he didn't know if he ever could. What was this sorrow that came with such thinking? Unsettled, he lifted a leg into the shower. His calves and thighs were already tightening. His shoulders and lower back were sore. Getting out of bed the next morning for work, he would surely ache.

Caring for the Dogs

Everything is overgrown. The truck's cooling engine pings and shishes its way to silence. Leaning into his seat, Wayne half expects to walk down to the mailbox and find another letter from the city about lawns and length restrictions and fines. The German Shepherd puppy in his hands wriggles, and he rubs its head as though it were a rabbit's foot. What lawn? Wayne thinks. Most of the grass has been crowded out by clover and moss. Dandelions gone to seed give the yard a hazy appearance. A few of the weeds up near the house have stems as thick as his thumb. He can see none of his basement windows.

The lawn isn't all that's gotten out of hand. Paint cans and power tools—including a circular saw, drill, and electric sander—extension cords, scrap molding, rusted toolboxes and fast food bags are crowded into the corners on the porch. In the driveway against the house rest snow shovels, milk crates, two extension ladders, old dining room chairs, sheets of plastic, buckets, and crumbling sheets of dry wall. Under a tarp, but partially exposed, the dresser Nancy had bought for their bedroom sits near the trashcans. He'd never been able to get it up the stairs. Near the back of the driveway a haphazard pile of rotted firewood threatens to spill into the neighbor's yard. A few stray pieces already have. He makes a mental note to call a chimney sweep before next fall. This year he wants to start having fires in the fireplace.

He makes other mental notes about where to start cleaning up. Even after a long day of snaking tampons out of drains and replacing hot water heaters, he feels that things could start to change. Ever since he picked up the puppy from a buddy's house, he's been feeling pretty good. Something feels right about holding a puppy, like waking after a long night's sleep.

The puppy works with his needle sharp teeth at Wayne's thumb. "Ouch, stop that," Wayne says, smiling. He opens his door. In the picture window, his other dogs—a Rottweiler, Doberman, and Pit Bull—shake their hind ends at the sight of him. The glass is fogged over from where they've been panting against it for weeks. When Wayne stands after setting the puppy into the high grass, the other dogs have lost their open-mouthed smiles. They stand still and tense in the window staring down at the new dog. The way they study it, they look both worried and intelligent. Wayne chuckles at them. The puppy doesn't notice, but stumbles around instead. Soon it turns back to Wayne.

"I'm not picking you up," he says. "You have to pee."

Watching the puppy, Wayne goes down to the mailbox. It's empty. Near the end of his driveway he finds a flattened pop cup from some fast food joint. He's seen it many times before, but today he picks it up and walks it back to the trashcan.

"Did you go?" he asks when he gets back to the puppy.

It starts a loping run, but gets tangled in the long grass and falls on its side. Wayne scoops it up. "This is where you pee. Outside," he says. He looks at the other dogs. They stand staring. Wayne starts up the porch steps.

"Hey Wayne, you got a second?"

He turns. His neighbor is coming across his freshly cut lawn and into Wayne's driveway. He wears a t-shirt, shorts, and expensive-looking running shoes.

"Hey," Wayne says. He doesn't really like the neighbor and can't remember his name. When the guy first moved in, he used to talk with Wayne any time he'd see him in the yard. If he were driving, he'd always hit his horn and wave. Within the last year though, he never even looks at Wayne's house. "Out running?" Wayne asks.

The neighbor looks down at himself. "Oh, yeah. Earlier." Looking up again, he eyes the puppy.

"I used to run, too," Wayne says, and catches the way the neighbor glimpses his big belly. "A long time ago," he adds. He'd run for nearly three months and had lost twenty-two pounds. But, when the gains came slower, he quit.

The neighbor says he gets out about three times a week.

Wayne doesn't say anything. A Saab goes by and beeps, and both men look towards the street. Wayne doesn't recognize the driver, but his neighbor waves and smiles. When Wayne and the neighbor look at each other again they are quiet.

"Hey," the neighbor finally says, "I don't know if you know it or not, but your dogs bark quite a bit when you're gone."

"Do they?" Wayne asks. He sees movement in the neighbor's house. Someone is standing a few feet back from the open parlor window. He guesses that it's the neighbor's wife.

"Yeah," the neighbor says. "Pretty loud, too."

Wayne looks at his house. He didn't know that the dogs barked so much, and he feels guilty. The neighbor has a toddler. "I keep a few windows open for them. For air," Wayne says. "I could close them. That would block the sound some."

"That would help," the neighbor says.

Wayne nods. "Alright," he says. He guesses that the neighbor is going to walk away. The puppy squirms in his hands.

"We use a service," the neighbor starts, "for our cats when we go on trips. I think the woman has a dog-walking service too for people who work all day. You want her number?"

Wayne thinks about it for a few seconds but guesses that something like that would get expensive. "No," he says.

"Big dogs like that need to get out," the neighbor says. He scratches the hair at the back of his head. "Do they ever get out for walks?"

"Yeah, I take them for walks," Wayne says, though he never does. He wants to punch the neighbor in the mouth.

"It's none of my..." the neighbor starts but then stops. "Anyway, yeah, if you'd close the windows I think that would help some."

Wayne nods and watches the neighbor cross back over his own lawn and disappear up his driveway. Screw you, he thinks, but when he turns towards his own house, he sees the dogs and feels bad that he doesn't walk them. I will tonight, he thinks. Good long walk tonight.

Opening the door, Wayne has to kick the dogs back. "Settle down!" he shouts. The puppy wriggles deeper into the crook of his arm and buries its face. "Just let me get in the damn door!" Driving the dogs back, he realizes that he forgot to buy dog food again. Just the night before he'd had to feed them two pounds of raw hamburger and half a loaf of white bread. He doesn't know what he'll give them tonight.

The dogs wriggle, yelp, and make small leaps. Their nails click frantically on the hardwood floor. The Rottweiler looks on the verge of a seizure and then a puddle grows under its hind legs.

"No!" Wayne shouts. He swings his foot and catches the dog in the ribs. It growls a warning. "Don't you growl at me."

The dogs crash after him from the living room into the kitchen. When he opens the back door, they charge out. "Go eat some of them squirrels," he shouts after them. A few weeks back he'd come across the remains of a nest of baby rabbits that they'd found and devoured. The soft tufts of fur blew around in the yard for a few days.

Going back into the living room with paper towel, Wayne sets the puppy down, wipes up the urine, and then collapses onto the couch. The blinking light of the answering machine catches his eye. He guesses that it's the city. They've been leaving messages lately, getting on him about the condition of the house. They talk about property values. Wayne watches the puppy instead of thinking about the house. Something about its haphazard darting and zigzagging lightens his mood. Instead of turning on the television, he turns on a light in a nearby room, guessing that there might be something for the puppy to play with.

The single bulb hanging from the ceiling illuminates the studs and lath of the walls. Most of the rooms in the house look like this. Piles of old plaster in the corners, dust, but mostly emptiness. This room was going to be Nancy's knitting room, but Wayne finds no balls of yarn. He looks around before turning off the light. They'd been so excited when they'd bought the big place, though Nancy later said that they'd only bought it because they couldn't have a baby together. Every room needed work, and Wayne had jumped right in with the demolition. He'd enjoyed swinging the sledgehammer and prying with the crowbar. The huge slabs that sprang from the walls and exploded on the floors gave a real satisfaction. But, after a solid month of working every night, he began to take breaks. Sometimes a two-day break would stretch into a two-week break. The break he took for Christmas lasted until April. It got to the point that the house was all he and Nancy ever talked about, and they yelled more than talked. Before the next Christmas, she had already moved into an apartment of her own.

In a small burst of energy after the New Year, he had finished the demolition, though not the cleanup. He called Nancy, but she told him that she didn't think they could work things out. They'd said too many things that they couldn't take back. He'd also heard that she'd started seeing someone else. Somewhere along the way, their relationship had come down with the plaster, and now lay in some irredeemable heap. So, after nearly two years of gutting the place, he wasn't sure where to begin to put it all back together. He'd started with the idea of dry walling the rooms, but it all seemed too big for him. He abandoned everything the day the divorce papers arrived.

Looking at the room now, Wayne can see why Nancy had to leave him. I let everything go to hell, he thinks. I should have finished what I started. Then moments later he thinks that she could have supported him more. She expected me to work every night. He gets angry. I was already killing myself all day in peoples' goddamn basements. Leaks, busted pipes, backed up drains. He flips the switch and the room goes black. You don't just walk out when things get tough, he thinks.

For a while he lies on the floor and wrestles the puppy with one hand. It bites and yips and treats his hand as though it were another puppy. Wayne gets lost in the play but soon is startled by the sound of crunching gravel. Someone has pulled into the driveway. He wonders if it's the police—they've come before about the lawn—but the knock he finally hears is too timid for an officer. The dogs in the backyard start barking.

"Jared?" Wayne says, opening the door to his son. The young man wears a uniform from a local ten-minute oil change place. *Jared* is stitched in red in his name patch. The hand he offers Wayne to shake is dirty. He looks older, as though he's twenty-eight instead of eighteen.

"It's been awhile, Dad," Jared says.

Wayne invites him in and shows him the new puppy. Jared stretches his long body out on the floor and begins to play with it just as Wayne had been.

"Nothing like a new pup," Wayne says. He figures it's been at least a year since he's seen Jared.

Jared doesn't say anything, but keeps playing with the puppy. Wayne offers him a beer.

"Dad, I'm not twenty-one."

"You think I don't know that? It's just a beer—in my own house."

Jared says he'll take the beer. He rolls the bottle between his hands, but doesn't take a drink. "I came over to ask you something." He talks very seriously.

Wayne's guts warm uncomfortably, and he wonders if Jared is going to bring up Frank, Wayne's oldest son. Frank is only an hour away in the medium-security prison in Standish, but Wayne hasn't made the drive in over two years. Who ever told the stupid sonuvabitch that breaking into peoples' houses would be a good idea? Wayne was already out of the house and starting a new life with Nancy by the time Frank started getting into real trouble. His decisions were his own, he thinks. A time comes when they're not your responsibility anymore.

"What's on your mind?" Wayne asks. He picks up the puppy. The other dogs have been barking since Jared knocked on the door.

"There's something I am really thinking about doing—something kinda big."

Wayne waits.

"I don't even like to say it, though, because every time I do people knock it apart." Jared sets the beer bottle on the floor and runs both hands through his long hair. He exhales.

"Just tell me."

Jared explains that he's been dating a girl, Tracy, for the last four months. They are in love. He wants to ask Tracy to marry him. Her uncle has a furniture factory in Tennessee and has promised Jared a job on the line. They feel they are ready to really start their lives together, even have kids.

"Do you want to work in a furniture factory?" Wayne asks. "Working on a line isn't easy."

"I don't know. I guess that doesn't matter, really. We just know we want to spend the rest of our lives together." He rubs his face.

Wayne knows immediately what he has to tell him. He's too young. He doesn't know what he's doing. He's probably not even really in love with the girl. Slow down. Give it more time. Don't be in such a hurry. This will be a big mistake. He guesses that this Tracy is the first girl Jared's ever slept with.

And, I gotta tell him about the job, Wayne thinks. A job can look really good for a while—until it pulls you in and there's no way out.

Jared stares at the puppy. He rings his hands. The way he concentrates, he looks as though he might be praying. But who the hell am I to tell him he shouldn't do this? Wayne then thinks. I was nineteen when I married Sharon. Sure, things fell to shit, but that doesn't mean Jared and this Tracy can't make things work. He realizes he was at his happiest when he and Sharon were starting off. He remembers their little apartment—just the two of them and furniture handed down from their families. Then he thinks about the first trailer they bought, watching Jared crawl on the floor, Frankie toddling. Looking up from the boys, he and Sharon would smile at each other, as though to say, "Look what we made from our love." Everything was right about those early times.

"How old are you?" Wayne asks.

"Nineteen."

In the backyard, the dogs bark steadily, more urgently. Wayne ignores them. "And you said you guys want to have kids?"

Jared nods.

"Nothing like a baby," Wayne says. He remembers how some nights he would stand at the boys' cribs and stare at them. They had so much promise. Still, I should tell the boy what he needs to hear, he thinks. Tell him that all of this could probably turn out a lot worse than it looks right now. Jared looks pale, as if hearing what he needs to hear one more time is going to kill him. But why should I have to play the heavy? Wayne thinks. Maybe he just really needs someone to believe in this with him. He stands up. "You should marry her," he announces.

Jared looks up. After a moment he smiles. "You're the only one who's said that."

The puppy bites Wayne's thumb again. "Ouch. Damn it." He puts his thumb in his mouth, talks around it. "I just remember what you're feeling. It feels good—the way you feel about her right now."

Jared nods, still smiling.

Wayne feels good too, light even. He lifts the puppy above him with both hands. "What do you think, boy? You want to be ring bearer?"

Jared laughs. Then he sits still on the couch, though he looks more like he's floating than sitting. "I've got to go," he says after a moment. "I want to see Tracy."

"Are you asking her now?"

"I think I might."

When they stand, Jared hugs Wayne. It's a small, awkward hug. But then Wayne sets the puppy on the floor and picks Jared up in a huge bear hug. They laugh.

Wayne watches him go down the porch steps and get into his car. It's an older car, rusted out at the bottoms of the doors, but it sounds okay when it turns over. Jared waves before backing into the street and driving away.

Out on the porch, Wayne can hear the dogs clearly. He looks over at the neighbor's house. Better let them in, he thinks. Before going in he gathers up an armload of fast food bags from the porch.

Opening the back door, he whistles for the dogs. "Come on, boys!" They charge into the house, knocking each other into the doorframe like the Three Stooges. "Jesus Christ, settle down," Wayne says, laughing. As soon as they get past him, he turns and runs into the living room behind them. All three are circled stiffly around the puppy, sniffing it as it whimpers.

The Rotweiller growls and Wayne kicks it in the rump. Then it turns and snaps at his foot. "Oh, you settle down tough guy." He scoops up the puppy. "Are you guys that worried about him?"

He sits on the couch while the dogs pace around looking for napping spots. They growl warnings when they pass each other, and Wayne laughs at them. He pictures Jared sliding into Tracy's driveway and jumping out of his car into the risen dust of the gravel. Probably blonde, Wayne thinks, and then imagines Tracy stepping out onto her porch as Jared sprints towards her.

"What?" she asks. "God, why are you smiling like that?"

"He said he thinks we should get married."

"What do you think?" she asks.

"I agree with him."

Tracy drops forward off the porch and falls into Jared's arms. He holds her up and spins her.

I could even help out with the wedding, Wayne thinks. Pay for the booze or something.

The puppy kicks in its sleep and Wayne looks down. It's just a small blackness in his lap, and he's surprised by how quickly night came on. The light on the answering machine pulses like a small, arrhythmic heart. Standing, he presses the button and then walks with the puppy into the kitchen. He guesses that he'll try to make dinner instead of buying fast food. After dinner he'll try to move some of the plaster out of the rooms. Or maybe he'll walk the dogs.

The answering machine beeps sharply. "Hello, Wayne? This is Sharon." Wayne freezes with his hand on the handle to the pots and pans cupboard. "I'm not really sure why, but Jared is going to come talk to you. He's met some girl and they're thinking of getting married. God knows why, but he wants to know what *you* think. Please, whatever you do, talk sense to him. You probably don't know it, but he's got a scholarship to take art classes at the community college. He's good, Wayne. He's really good. They are going to pay for everything—books, tuition... He can't blow this chance by running off and getting married. Just tell him what he needs to hear." The message stops.

Wayne's head seems to fill with ether. His body, lead. He closes the door and pulls himself up to the counter, where he leans most of his weight. "Oh shit," he says. "Sonuvabitch." He wonders if he could still get a hold of Jared before he talks to Tracy, but then realizes that there's no way. He stays at the counter, rubbing the heel of his hand into his eyes. Why the hell didn't I just tell him what he needed to hear? Why don't I ever do the right thing? A few minutes pass. Jesus Christ, he thinks, how the hell am I supposed to know he's got a goddamn scholarship? Nobody tells me anything.

No longer hungry, he walks heavily into the dark living room. He wants to erase the message. He wants to erase all of this and get back to what he was feeling earlier. Briefly, he is aware of something crunching under his boot. As he realizes that it's a dog's paw, a sharp pain circles his ankle. "Goddamnit!" he screams, dropping the puppy. It yelps.

The jawing pressure around his ankle does not let up, and Wayne guesses that the Rotweiller has him. "No, Butch! No!" He tries to pry at the dog's mouth with his hands, but is unable to open the grip. The dog clenches and releases rhythmically as though trying to gnaw to the bone.

"Goddamnit, let go!" Wayne tries to open the jaws again, but can't. He starts punching the dog repeatedly on its snout.

It takes a few punches, releases the ankle, and then clamps onto the fist. Wayne screams. The release of pressure to his ankle serves to double the pain there, and he falls down to his knees. Now the Rotweiller attacks more determinedly. Its bites land around Wayne's arms as he tries to cover his head. After growling and barking, the other dogs join in. "No!" Wayne shouts. "It's me! It's me!"

The puppy whines from a corner of the room.

Sleepwalker

Martin can still hear the way Vickie screamed that night when they'd set the bone. He winces. She was just a little girl, then. Downstairs, pots and pans knock against each other. The cupboard closes. A passing car smears a phantom window over his walls. It leaves behind darkness and the gray outlines of things in the room. Now Vickie must be at least in her late thirties. Forties?

She goes through the silverware drawer. Martin sighs. He doesn't know why his daughter is home now. He doesn't want to know.

Sleepwalking. They really didn't know anything about it. Martin believed it was important not to wake her. Doctors said that there was really no danger in it. Disoriented. Confused. That's all she would be. She'd come around. They'd also heard that she couldn't hurt herself. He and Charlotte would lie in bed listening to her downstairs picking up her toys or searching for something. Whispering and giggling over what she might be doing, they held each other. Then one night she pulled the television down on herself and broke her arm.

"Can't really say how long she'll do this," the doctor said. He explained that it usually ended around twelve years old, but it could go longer.

Vickie lay in Charlotte's arms, already sleeping. Her tiny arm disappeared into the cast. Charlotte asked if there was anything they could do.

"Put up a gate so she can't get downstairs easily. Move things so she doesn't trip. Make sure she gets good sleep every night. Naps maybe." The doctor pulled the curtain back. The E.R. was noisy. Screaming. Crying. Complaining. Talking. Medical babble.

"Isn't there any way to treat it," Martin had asked, "some pill or something?"

"If it gets really bad, there are short-acting tranquilizers, but hold off on that for now. Just help her take care of that arm. There's really no quick fix." He wished them a safe drive home. He left the curtain open.

"Charlotte? Are you awake?" Martin asks, uneasy with his memories.

No answer.

He reaches for the back of her thigh, but can't find her in the sheets and blankets of the king-sized bed. More cars drone past.

"Why is she home again? I don't remember her telling us why."

He stares into the blackness above their bed. "Do you remember the first time she came back home? She stayed for a year. Remember? That phone call in the middle of the night. I drove because they said they'd keep her at the hospital until I got there." He rubs his eyes. "One semester before she was going to finish."

He pulled open the curtain. Vickie sat on the edge of a hospital bed. At least twenty pounds lighter, she stared at her feet. Stringy hair hanging down. Skinny arms coming out of the thin hospital gown. Harsh fluorescent light.

"Daddy," she said, "please don't say anything." She didn't look up.

"Why would I say anything? I've only been on the road for three hours to take a two-hour trip. I'm damn near night blind, but maybe being on drugs made you forget that." He tried to stop. "A near overdose. That's what a doctor was telling me on the phone at midnight about you. So why should I say anything?"

"Daddy, please."

"Daddy? All of a sudden, daddy? Vickie what... I mean, I wanted to come here someday to see you in a gown, but I was hoping for a graduation gown."

She raised her hands to her face and convulsed with sobbing. A nurse had to walk her to the car. Then, three hours of silence.

Martin breathes through his mouth. He stares into the dark ceiling. "I shouldn't have said that to her. I was just ... I was angry. But, I shouldn't have talked like I did."

He knows what his wife would say. "Vickie was not an easy daughter. So you said things. Still, you let her stay at the house for over a year. That's what matters."

"Of course I let her stay. I was angry, but this is home. And, she got help. Remember the meetings?" He reaches again for Charlotte. His hand touches the remote control for the television.

Downstairs, a closet door opens.

"Did you hear that? I think Vickie's home again. Still sleepwalking. The doctors said she'd outgrow it. So much she never outgrew." He listens. "Do you know why she's home, Charlotte? I don't remember why this time? What does she need? Money? Just a place to stay? It must have been when I went walking after dinner. Is that when she told you why she's home?"

He pulls the remote from under the sheets. "I'm going to turn this on. Do you mind? I just can't sleep with her down there making that noise."

Television light flickers in the room. Martin tries to follow the programs, but can't. The plots lose him. The punch lines on the late night talk shows aren't funny. He laughs a few times, but only because he recalls the antics of Johnny Carson's program. "Now he was funny," he used to tell Vickie. "These new guys don't know how to be funny—only filthy. And weird." He turns off the television, and the room goes black. It lightens slowly.

Downstairs, the den door squeaks on its hinges. He vaguely remembers Vickie being home again for some reason. "I was terrible the last time," he says, hoping that the television woke Charlotte. "The last time she came home to stay I said terrible things—things a father shouldn't say."

"Not every father has Vickie for a daughter. She wasn't easy," Charlotte used to say.

"I know, I know ... but, still. The next morning she was gone. I remember that night so clearly."

He had gone downstairs. Vickie was making a sandwich. She made one for him, and then they watched television. They found a channel showing highlights from the Johnny Carson show.

"Now this stuff is funny," Martin said. He laughed and pointed and looked over at Vickie for her reaction.

"I like Letterman better," she returned, her mouth full of sandwich.

"Letterman?" Martin hissed. "Throwing pencils around? His stupid faces? That's not funny."

She finished her sandwich. "Why are we even watching this? This isn't even a show. This is a commercial, Dad. They want you to buy their tapes. Do we have to sit here and watch a commercial like it's a show? Can we see if something else is on?"

Martin was quiet for a moment, but he didn't change the channel. "You know what else isn't funny?" he asked. "Throwing your life away isn't funny," he answered.

"I'm going to bed." She stood.

"Not in my house you're not," Martin said. "Not with my bread and peanut butter and jam in your mouth, you're not. You're going to listen. For once, you're going to listen."

She turned towards him and crossed her arms.

He cleared his throat. Then he asked her why she left Roger. She said she didn't know. He asked if she didn't think that filing for a divorce was a little rash. She said she didn't know. He asked her what, if anything, did she know.

"I know this isn't helping. I know I'd just like to go to bed."

"Do you think you can just sleep this off? You're thirty-two years old. You had a house, a husband who took care of you—a husband who was going to help you go back to school. You just walked away from it. Why?"

"I told you I don't know."

Martin stared at the television. "You don't know," he said. "That boy calls every day. He asks me why. *Me.* What am I supposed to tell him?"

Vickie uncrossed her arms. She sighed. "I'm just going to go to bed, okay?" She turned around and started towards the stairs.

"I'm going to tell you something," Martin said.

She stopped, but didn't turn around.

"I've never prayed. But after this—when you had what everyone wants. And now you're throwing it away ... everything, your whole life—like it's not a gift. I prayed last night. I prayed to something or someone that you start to do something right. I..." He looked up, stopped. "Okay, go ahead. Run up to your room! Smoke a cigarette and blow the smoke out your window like you did when you were a teenager under this roof. That will make everything better. A little girl. That's all you'll ever be!" He was yelling up the stairs after her until her door slammed.

"When I came to bed that night you didn't say anything," he says to Charlotte. Then he waits. "You were kind, but I know I was wrong. I wasn't a good father. The next morning she was gone. Not even a note."

"Vickie was never an easy daughter," Charlotte used to say. "You do what you can. You leave the door open. What else can you do?"

"I was a terrible father," he says.

He'd said it before, but Charlotte always reminded him that even after that last time Vickie called three days later. He begged her to come back, and she did.

"But still," he says, "a father doesn't say such things. Such venom."

He reaches around. His hand touches upon the television remote control. He turns it on. He finds nothing he can follow. He hits the button again. Darkness.

"Charlotte? Charlotte? Do you think I was a terrible father? I said such things. I have my father's mouth. I just think that I pushed her away—that it's my fault that she turned out this way. Will she ever come around?"

He listens. Nothing. He decides he'll let his wife sleep.

A drawer opens and then closes downstairs.

Martin sits up. "Charlotte, did you hear that? There's someone in the house?" He remembers something dimly. "Maybe it's Vickie. She's home, isn't she? She came home again."

He listens. The house pings and pops in the walls.

"I think she's sleepwalking. She never outgrew it. Remember, like the doctor said?" He listens. "She's so quiet down there." He sits up and puts his feet on the floor. "Do you remember the television? Her little arm?" He listens again. "Why is she here? It's so quiet downstairs now. What's she doing?"

He stands up. "I'm going to check on her," he whispers over the bed.

The stairs creak under his feet. He thinks he hears Charlotte coming behind him, but he has to concentrate on the steps to keep his balance. He stops on the landing and can hear Vickie talking in the kitchen.

"Yeah, fine I guess," she says. "Fine as can be."

She pauses.

"Sometimes to me, but it's in and out." She's quiet for a moment. "Yeah. More to himself, really. Or, I guess to her. That's what it sounds like. Like he thinks she's still here."

Martin smiles. "Do you hear her? Sleepwalking. Remember the doctor talking about the talking—the sleep talk babble?" He turns, but Charlotte is not on the stairs. He will tell her in the morning. He takes the last few steps.

He moves towards the corner. "About three weeks already," Vickie says. Kitchen light shines off a wall in the dining room. "I'll stay until whenever. I just want him to be in his own house for as long as possible."

Martin grins, snorting a tiny laugh through his nose. Beginning to turn the corner, he stops. He's not sure he's ready to know why his daughter is home. He remembers something dark. Then he forgets and turns into the light.

That Which We Are

When I'd texted Holly to ask how long she was thinking, she took her time answering, and then only texted back, "uncertainly temporary." That was three days earlier. Her gray-bubbled message was still there on the bottom of my screen next to the tiny thumbnail of her picture. The photo was from some trip she'd taken with a divorced girlfriend not too long ago and in it she's smiling like crazy, something I hadn't seen in person in a long time. That she'd switched to that picture still pissed me off.

The glow from my screen and the beam from my father's roving flashlight were the only sources of light in his near-freezing kitchen. I could see my breath in the faint luminescence from my phone. The blizzard raging outside rattled the window pane above the sink.

"Do you even hear it out there?"

He ignored my question.

I pressed the button and put the phone to sleep. I didn't guess that Holly would answer even if I did message. Even if I did tell her I had a real crisis here. If the roles were reversed, and she texted me, I know I wouldn't have responded. Truthfully she probably would have responded, but I didn't need a rundown of every way I was handling all of this wrong.

My father's frantic light flashed around the room. He was opening and closing drawers and making small noises of triumph each time he found something he thought might be useful. He was filling his leather tool bag.

He held up a wire stripper that I'd seen him use many times before. It glowed in his palm in a halo of flashlight.

"They're not going to let you take that bag on—" He turned and flashed the light into my face. I shielded my eyes. "Jesus Christ, come on Dad, you're blinding me here."

"Sorry," he said. He turned the light toward the zippered opening of his bag and dropped the wire stripper where it fell to join his compression crimper, screwdrivers, torpedo level, pliers, measuring tape, hex-key set, adjustable wrench, cable ripper, and receptacle tester. The beam from his flashlight lit up the heart-red casing of his voltage meter just before he zipped the bag closed.

He'd told me about his ridiculous plan over the phone earlier that evening when I called to see how he was holding up in the storm. He said his power had been out for hours, but that really wasn't on his mind. Instead he started talking about Puerto Rico and something about the double whammy of hurricanes Irma and Maria. "It's been three months," he said, "and half of them still don't have electricity." When I told him he was 72 years old with congestive heart failure, he didn't respond other than to say "not advanced." He said he was sitting in his house feeling the air getting colder and grousing to himself about having no television when it suddenly hit him. "I'm an electrician with 44 years' experience," he said. With none of his home repair programs to watch, he told me that he was holding a picture of my mom, staring at her, when the idea came to him. "It was like a vision," he said.

My father didn't talk that way. Ever.

I hung up and white-knuckled through the squalls over to his place and nosed the front end of my truck into the 16 plus inches of snow in his driveway. Even with the storm-wrecked roads and the wind threatening to spin me out into a snowbank, I drove with one hand. In the other hand I was holding my phone with my thumb hovering above Holly's number. She'd said something once about maybe my dad had some signs of dementia. I thought she'd have some advice on how to handle this, but by the time I was in my old man's driveway, I hadn't pulled the trigger on calling her, so I didn't.

Lately our fights had been about money. I thought we didn't have enough, and Holly wanted to support causes. I'd started finding charges on the credit card statement to liberal political campaigns. We had agreed to talk about any miscellaneous spending.

"Why didn't you just ask me?"

"Because I already knew you'd say no," she said.

I asked if that was her idea of logic. "I would say no, so you figure the best route is to do it anyway?"

She looked at the floor for a moment and then looked up at me. "When will we have enough, Marcus? When will it be enough money for you?" Her eyes looked a way I'd never seen them before, like I could fall into them. "We just don't see things the same way," she said. "In times like this you can't just do nothing."

I'd heard enough. "That doesn't make your way the right way," I said and then walked out of the room.

Dad lifted his bag from the floor and set it on the kitchen counter next to a backpack he'd told me he'd stuffed with clothes and his pills. He turned off his flashlight. "Weird grid," he said. "There's power across the street and with the neighbors behind me but, this side of the street, nothing."

I took a long breath and exhaled it slowly. "Dad, do you even have a ticket?" The room was lit dimly by a yellowed light coming through the windows.

He shook his head. Then he patted his jacket pocket. "I have my passport, though." He said he'd needed to get one when he took his cruise from Edinburgh to Dublin. "That was a trip your mother had always wanted to take." He shook his head. "Really, any trip. I always told her no, that we couldn't—"

"Jesus, Dad, you don't need a passport for Puerto Rico. And, you're serious that you don't even have your plane ticket?" I shook my head. "You should probably just sleep on this whole plan."

He told me he'd slept long enough . "I can get a ticket at the airport. "

Trying to glow through the static of snowfall, the streetlight across the road looked like a dull globe of sun through a morning fog.

I asked him if he'd even looked at it outside. "No planes are leaving tonight. Not in this."

He said he'd be fine at the airport, even for a few days. "I used to think about that," he said, rubbing his index finger over the bridge of his nose. "A person could live in an airport." He looked at me. "What? With ATMs, you could do it. They have all those restaurants. People are sleeping there all the time, so nobody would pay any attention. There's television. Bathrooms." He said some of the bigger ones even had showers and laundry facilities. Then, he laughed. "That'd be something, wouldn't it? Somebody could be living at an airport right now."

I stared at him for a moment. The only thing moving was the fog of our breath between us. His breathing was wheezy. "That what you want to do, Dad? You want to live at the airport now?"

He snapped his head as though coming out of a fugue. "What?" He turned towards his bags on the countertop. "No, I told you. I'm going to Puerto Rico to help with the power outage."

I watched him fussing with the bags, double-checking each of the zippers. He seemed like he was stalling or maybe uncertain of his own whereabouts. He looked frail and the jeans that had once fit him snuggly flapped around his skinny legs. My father was old, likely weak, and maybe losing his mind.

"Listen..." I started.

He turned to me. A few wisps of grey hair were long and resting over the crown of his head, like a ragged ghost of his comb-over from years before.

"Your mother had this tradition," he said. His voice was reedy, as though he might weep.

"Dad—"

He swatted a hand toward me. "Just listen, would ya." He said this was something my mother had done when she was single and had carried into the first years of their marriage. "She did it until Charles was around seven and you were about three."

A little something went through me at the mention of Charles' name. I wondered sometimes, even at 41 years old, what it would have been like to have him around to help out with Dad. Or just to have a brother to talk to like Holly had her sister. Charles died from leukemia when he was 13.

That was another thing with Holly and me. She wanted to have kids. I didn't. Not with all the desolating things that can happen to them. My parents were in counseling for years after Charles passed, just trying to stay together. When my mom died, my dad told me that all that counseling had been for me, which I never really knew how to take.

I sighed. "What did Mom do? Is this story even—"

"Listen." He pointed at me. "Every Christmas Eve," he started. Then, "Well, no ... I mean, first, it was all year. Like each month she would put aside money, maybe like 50 dollars a month."

I was pretty sure I knew where this was going. It was basic money management. You don't let Christmas shopping sneak up on you. You save up all year so it doesn't bust your budget or, worse, you put everything on a credit card. "I get it," I said. "Like a Christmas club."

He shook his head. "No, let me finish." He told me about how my mom would save this money throughout the year, sometimes nearly a thousand dollars. Then on Christmas Eve she would get in her car and drive around. "She'd find people working at gas stations or liquor stores or people working motel front desks." He told me that she'd go in with a greeting card. "Usually there'd be like 50 bucks inside. And she'd just hand the card to whoever was working. So this stranger, probably upset because they had to work Christmas Eve, would get this money, but then these beautiful cards, too, with inspirational quotes handwritten inside."

He looked into my face for a moment, his own face thinking: "'Don't allow your eyes to adjust to the lack of light,'" he said to me across the dusky kitchen. "'Instead, do something to illuminate the darkness.'" Snapping his fingers, he laughed. "I still remember it. I can't remember whether or not I took my pills this morning, but I remember that quote from one of her cards." He looked up toward the ceiling. "Must be nearly 40 years ago. Maybe more."

I recalled something about that being a thing with dementia, remembering the past better than the present.

Outside, the backup beeper of a snowplow pulsed high-pitched somewhere in a parking lot in the neighborhood. I'd heard on the radio that it was supposed to snow all night. "Dad—"

"I ruined it," he said.

"What?"

He shook his head. "That goddamn television." Then like flipping a switch he said something about needing to pack another pair of socks and wandered down the dark hallway towards his bedroom.

The television? His mind was going everywhere. The living room was just off of the kitchen. Its huge picture window looked out onto the back lawn. A neighbor's yard light reflecting off the snow filled the room with a jaundiced glow. Glancing in, I immediately saw what my father meant. A breath caught in my throat when I saw the lightning rod sticking out of the screen.

We'd had the television for years. It was one of the first large-screen deals before they'd developed the technology to make them flat. It was mounted in a faux-oak cabinet and must have weighed over 200 pounds. I'd offered Dad any number of times to replace it, but he didn't believe in getting rid of anything that still worked no matter how dim the brightness. In the months after my mom died, I drove over to my father's a couple nights a week for *Mad Money*. We didn't really talk, but he seemed content to have someone with him to watch Jim Cramer's antics. I didn't mind. I liked the show.

He'd have to replace the television now.

A year or so after my mother died, my father went through a period where he decided he was going to collect antiques related to electricity. He had a pretty good collection of old light bulbs, light switches, switchboards, wall mount brass plates and some single, double, and triple throw knife switches. The collection was a mishmash prioritized mainly by what he thought he could afford. Right near the end of his collecting phase, he found his favorite piece, a lightning rod. Its braided wrought iron base was sticking out of the television's screen shattered into a spider's web of cracks.

My father had lost his mind. I was sure of it. Pressing that number on my phone ... it was like an involuntary reaction, like flinching. Holly picked up after only two rings.

"Marcus?"

Something about hearing her voice ripped a seal in me. I started immediately with something about my father being in a dementia-induced fit. Even as I unloaded everything, I could hear the muffled sound of children in the background on her end. I wondered if maybe her sister had come into town with her kids and was visiting with her parents. If so, I was certain I was getting raked over the coals. Her sister was not by biggest fan and probably not the best ear for Holly while we were separated.

"It sounds like he's pretty determined," Holly said.

I told her I didn't know what to do. "I need you," I said. The words came out of me quietly, almost a whisper. A prayer. "I don't know how to deal with him like this. I'm worried he'll hurt himself."

She was quiet a moment. "Do you think he'd talk to me? Can you get him on the phone?"

The sound of children's voices grew louder and then softened again. A little girl's voice asked Holly something that I couldn't make out. Something about pizza.

"Where are you?" I asked.

She hesitated. Then she told me that she was at a hotel in Sterling Heights. "Janet lost power at her place, so I got us a room. Her house was getting cold. She didn't have anywhere to go. Her kids love swimming." The sound of laughing children spiked again.

"Janet?" Something hot raced up my spine. She was the divorced friend that Holly had taken a few girls' weekends with over the last few months. I didn't mind at first because she came home happy. Happy for a few hours, anyway. "What do you mean *you* got the room?"

"I mean I paid for the room. Blake took Janet back to court after Steinman's moved her to full-time. He got the child support cut in half, and things are tight for—"

"How did you pay for the room?"

"With the credit card, Marcus."

I squeezed my free hand into a fist, feeling my fingernails dig into my palm. "My credit card. So you mean I paid for the room."

"If that's the way you need to look at it, then yes, you and I paid." She sighed. "We're only staying the one night and—"

"So are we getting divorced or what? How long am I supposed to live with this 'uncertainly temporary' shit?"

The wind howled past the picture window. The door on the storage shed banged opened and closed in the gusts. Holly said nothing.

"Seriously, I thought you were staying at your folks to think things through. Not having a fucking pool party on my dime."

"I have a job, too," she said.

I exhaled a sound like a laugh. "Yeah, and sixty thousand dollars in student loans that we'll be paying down for the next—"

"Marcus," she said, her voice sharp and arresting, "you called me. About your dad. How do you want me to help with him?"

"Forget it. I'll handle it myself."

"Marc—"

I pressed the power button and killed the call.

A moment later, the door in the kitchen closed. It took me a minute to put together that my father had gone to the garage. I found him out there on a footstool, shining his flashlight above him with one hand and groping for the emergency release cord on the garage door opener with the other. His balance was already bad, and it wasn't helped by his thick parka and the backpack of clothes strapped over his shoulders. The stool wobbled under his feet.

"What the hell are you doing, Dad? You're going to break your neck."

He grabbed the plastic handle and pulled the cord. "There," he said. "Now open the door for me."

I walked over and pulled up on the handle, sending the door sliding up along its tracks. Snow cascaded onto the garage floor. "It has to be nearly two feet deep out there," I said.

He stood with his hand resting on the top of his Cadillac's open driver's door. "It's only a few miles to the airport."

I looked out into the blizzard-swept neighborhood and then back at him. "You won't get halfway down the driveway."

He looked at the storm for a moment. Then, he flipped up the fur-lined hood on his parka and closed the car door. He pulled his gloves tight on each hand. "Fine, I'll walk."

I walked over to him. "Jesus Christ, Dad. I think you're cracking up here. Do you even remember what you did to the television?"

He looked up at me from under the rim of the hood. "I remember."

I crossed my arms. "So what the hell was that about?"

His gaze dropped toward the floor. "I never should have bought that TV."

"What are you talking about now?" I asked, leaning against the Cadillac.

He took in a long breath and released it slowly. "Your mother, that last time ... she got the flu. Even a few days before Christmas, she knew there was no way she'd be able to get out of bed to give those cards out." He told me that they'd argued about it a few times earlier that fall. "I told her that we could use that money," he said. "She said we'd gotten by without it all year and it was meant for other people. 'It's something we can do that's bigger than us,' she said."

I shivered. The cold from the car had leached through my jacket.

He didn't look up from the floor. "She told me where she kept the money. She gave me the cards already filled out with the inspirational quotes. She wanted me to deliver them." He looked up at me and worried a hand over his pale chin. "I bought that television instead." He told me he threw the cards away. "Christmas morning, she came down and I had a big bow on the TV. You and your brother were so excited. That kinda made it feel like I'd done the right thing. I told your mother she wasn't the only one that could save up all year." He looked down again. "I never told her what I did."

I shrugged. "We did watch a lot of shows together on that set, Dad. Watched a lot of Tigers games and—"

He shook his head. "Doesn't matter. There's bigger things. You figure that out sitting by yourself day after day."

I reached out to touch his shoulder but then drew my hand back in.

"I was an idiot," he said. "The next year, I was after her all the time about that money. If we had a car repair or you boys needed something, I was always telling her that we should just use the Christmas Eve fund. I wore her down to the point that in

August she just gave it to me. Four hundred and eighty bucks. Said she didn't want to do it anymore anyway. That I was right about us needing it for the family." He looked up at me again with watery eyes. "She said, 'It's silly. I mean, giving money away. I don't know what I was thinking.'" He sniffed in a melancholy breath. "Kinda rips me up that I can still hear her voice saying it, you know. I made her feel stupid about wanting to be nice to other people."

He dabbed some tears from his cheek with the back of his glove. I don't think I'd ever seen him cry before, not even when my mother passed.

"I think you should stay here, Dad. I think we should get you to a doctor."

He looked into my face. His eyes looked steely, determined. "I'm not sick."

He pushed past me and started into the snow-clogged driveway. I didn't need this in my life. I bolted after him and grabbed his coat sleeve, stopping him and turning him toward me. The wind howled around us.

"I'm not letting you—"

He shoved me over with a strength I was surprised he still had. I lay in the snow looking up at him, his face haloed by his hood. He looked down at me for a moment. "Don't try to stop me again," he said and then turned and continued trudging down the driveway.

When I got to my feet, he was already in the road, making his way down a single pass that one of the city snowplows had made.

I brushed the snow from my palms and shoved my hands into my pockets. I called out to him above the storm. He kept going. The stubborn sonuvabitch. His silhouette slowly disappeared into the squalls, darkness, and distance.

The whole time my left hand was turning my phone over in my pocket. I was fighting the instinct to call Holly again. I shook my head. Enough of that. The first thing I really needed to do was already in play in my head. And the second.

I went back into my dad's house. Going to the basement, I turned off the water main. I didn't know how long he'd be gone. I didn't know how long the house would be without power. The last thing the place needed was a burst water pipe.

I started upstairs and turned on each faucet until they sputtered dry. I flushed the toilets. I was thinking the whole time.

Without a hose, I had to empty the hot water heater into a bucket. I opened the valve by soft degrees. Watching it drain, I punched a number into my cell. I stood in the darkness of the cold basement, my eyes having grown used to the lack of light, listening to my phone ring. When the call was answered, I told her what I needed.

"Yes," I said, "cancel both cards." I shook my head. "No, just send one replacement."

I lingered awhile then, how long I'm not sure, in my father's basement. I stayed until even the drip from the drained water heater stopped. The cold from the concrete penetrated into my soles and crept its way chillingly up through my legs. I'd worked in bitter temperatures enough times in the past to know that it was a chill that would stay with me a long time, even after a hot shower.

I touched the screen on my phone and went to texts. Studying the thumbnail picture, I ignored the face of my wife's divorced friend. It was Holly's smiling face I wanted to see. There'd been a time that I could make her smile like that. How long ago it'd been, I didn't remember. I just remembered there'd been a time that making that face smile was all that had mattered to me.

I set the phone upside down against my thigh. I was in darkness again, my eyes having adjusted to the small light of the screen.

I picked up the phone, scrolled, and then tapped an icon.

"Yes, hello," I said. "I just called a bit ago about ordering a replacement card. I'd like to cancel that." We finished up the necessary business to reverse the request.

Hanging up, I thought of my father out there in the storm trudging toward the airport. Turning on my phone's flashlight, I ran up the basement steps and out the front door towards my truck, which I would use to drive him the rest of the way following the halo of my headlights.

Distance

In the distance, the muffler fades, but grumbles at the edges of earshot. He holds the stop sign, cold metal in his fist, and with his other hand pulls his ankle up, stretching his quad. He counts and then switches hands, legs. He lets go of the sign. He rubs his palms and fingers over his arms vigorously. He hugs himself. Closing his eyes and then bending, he reaches towards his feet and stretches his calves. The joints behind his knees tingle and burn. His house is behind him, only two driveways back. He wants to rise out of this stretch and just run. He wants it to be easy tonight. Sighing, he turns and looks towards the second floor.

His daughter's light glows. Damn it. Still crying. Her fever was slight, but she'd thrown up. Maybe she is throwing up. Or maybe a phone call woke them. He shudders. But, no, she wouldn't. He'd told her not to.

His wife's words come as though she were saying them to him now: "Every night, jogging? You have to?" He told her it wasn't every night. It was every other night. "And I should get to do something, shouldn't I?" She didn't answer. "An hour," he said. "I'm gone an hour. I have this one thing I like. Don't make me feel guilty." She shook her head. "Fine," she said.

He touched her arm. "I'll be one hour. I just want to get an hour in."

He changed slowly, tied his shoes slowly. The stairs creaked when she brought Chelsea up to bed. She'll sleep now, he thought. They'll both sleep. The fever will come down. She'll sleep. He padded down the back stairs to the back door. Closing it, he heard Chelsea cry again. Can't be. Must have been the hinges. He locked the door. He put the key under his driver's side tire like he did every time, so as not to have it bumping against his leg in the loose pocket of his shorts.

At least a minute passes. Her light stays on. What can I do? One person can change her if she's thrown up. One person can hold her until she sleeps. A second person adds nothing. I'd be in the way. "Why are you back here?" she'd ask. "Just run," she'd say.

A silhouette moves past the blind, bouncing slightly. They'll be fine. They'll be sleeping when I get back. She doesn't need me. He turns and launches into the first few steps that he hopes to turn into five miles. Maybe six.

The knee. It clicks and aches. "Not good to run on this," a doctor said after listening to the clicking. He pumped the shin again and the joint clicked. "It's bad in the long run." He smiled at the doctor. "Nice pun," he said. The doctor told him he wasn't kidding. He mentioned surgery, a long recovery. Maybe a life-long limp. "Fine, fine," he said. "I'll stop. No more running." But he didn't quit. He'd always run. It kept him young, thin. Everything else was easier with youth and thinness. The knee never hurt other times.

In the morning. It hurts in the morning. That's it. And sometimes on stairs. He changes his gait and favors the knee. For a few blocks it's a limping jog. His breaths are gulping, arrhythmic. He thinks about the knee and his breathing and wonders why he does this. He considers what he'd have gained by staying home.

He hits the street that marks his first mile. Something's changed. He runs normally. The knee is fine after the mile of warm up. Just needs that warm up, he thinks, smiling. It's fine after that warm up.

The knee is behind him. He doesn't think about it anymore. It does what it's supposed to do. For the first mile it's always the knee. The next mile he can look around. His breathing, too, becomes easier. He knows now that he can keep this up. Big breaths through his mouth lift his rib cage. He's just running. Free. He doesn't have to think about breathing. The sweat, rising to the surface, warms his face. His feet drum a pulse against the sidewalk.

He knows the homes that have dogs. They bark, but he does not jump. The streetlights are spaced out equally. In the halo of each, a tree's limbs splinter through the light in stark relief. The neighborhood is almost silent except for the cars. They slow to a stop. They idle briefly. They speed up through intersections. They're gone. Some come at him, flashing bright light over him. The darkness he is left in after the flash of light is darker. His eyes adjust slowly. He has to watch his step for this mile. The town is old and the roots of the old trees crack and hunch the sidewalks. I could easily twist an ankle, he thinks. He watches for cracks.

Ahead, a shadow moves. There's sound. He makes sense of it—someone dragging a garbage can down to the curb. When he passes the can, the person is gone, their house already dark. She and Chelsea are probably asleep by now. Why wouldn't they be? They don't need me. Not for a small fever like that.

He thinks he hears it. Maybe a street or so behind him. He slows, but doesn't hear the muffler. Every night this guy. He just drives around and around? What kind of person lurks around the streets like that? Unsettling people. What is there in that?

Everything is loose, flowing. The run is good now. He remembers why he likes it and why he goes every other night.

Everything around him goes black. A streetlight out. He wants to watch his feet, make certain of his footing, but his eyes are pulled to the windows of the houses going past, now somehow brighter. Quick glimpses. Most are living room windows. Bookshelves. Plants. Lamps. Couches. And always televisions. Always on.

The bedroom window of a one-story ranch glows ahead of him. The Venetian blinds are not yet closed. He studies the lit room expectantly. And, as though he wished it there, he sees flesh. Then, the stark white of panties and bra. She's moving in front of a closet, either dressing or undressing. He slows. Stops. He's outside in the darkness, and she is inside in the bright light. She can't see me. He waits. He breathes heavily.

She stands in front of a closet. Slowed like this, not flashing by, she is heavier, her skin folding slightly around her waistline and over her bra strap. His wife looks this way ever since Chelsea was born. I should go home, he thinks. It would mean something that I come home early—tell her that I thought of her. He waits, watches. He can't move away from the flesh in the window. How often is something like this going to happen to me?

A screen door closes across the street. "Gypsy? Here, Gypsy!" a woman calls.

He lurches into his run again, and his knee twinges. He looks back, and a woman's silhouette moves near the silhouette of bushes around a porch. She bends over and then calls again.

Cat or a dog. He slows into a pace he will be able to maintain.

Was she getting dressed or undressed? Would he have seen her, like a husband watches his wife from a bed, casual with her nudity? She might have done anything. He teases himself with the idea of going around a few blocks and coming back to her window. Just to see. I could. There's no reason why I couldn't. He tempts himself more with the idea, and it's not long before he comes to the fire hydrant that he knows to be the second mile marker.

This time, he's certain he hears it. Idling. Crawling along the pavement. If you're going to be a god damn pervert, fix your muffler. The car comes down the street that he just crossed. He hears it behind him. The street he's on is long and straight. He jogs through pools of streetlight, the edges of which blend into each other. Here there's only a half-darkness. The car creeps into the intersection of the cross street behind him. The muffler grumbles.

He sees me. He's watching me. But let him watch. What's he going to do?

His heart beats in his throat. He glances over his shoulder. The car idles, unmoving, in the intersection, now two streets back. It's an older car. Long. What the hell is it with this guy? I mean, this is kicks?

Stopping directly under a streetlight, he turns around. He stares towards the car. The silhouette of the driver turns towards him. He waits, but the car doesn't move. He shrugs his hands into the empty air, juts his jaw. "What?" he shouts, voice cracking.

The car grumbles away and disappears behind the corner of a house. He listens until the muffler is gone.

Asshole. Every night with this guy. He listens again, but hears nothing. He limps into his jog, knee clicking. I can't keep stopping, he thinks, wincing. It's a few blocks before the knee starts to warm up again.

The doctor held the knee from behind. He lifted it slightly, as though to show it to him. "It's a fragile thing from the beginning," he said. Ten pounds of pressure can snap a good one, he explained. "And yours. It could just blow out, just give." He held it like something precious.

The knee warms up again and feels okay. Doctors. He shakes his head. In a few blocks he enters the city's running and bike path. The sign says that the path is off limits after ten o'clock, but he knows that nobody enforces it. The sign is to keep teenagers away. And, if he'd have been a teenager, he'd have come anyway. He never paid much attention to signs.

He leaves the streets and the houses behind. He won't have to worry about his footing because the path is always smooth. And dark. Sweat drips from his face. Sweat, now soaked in his sweatshirt, cools and rests against his skin uncomfortably. A ghost of pain haunts the knee. Stopped too many times, he thinks.

In the darkness he remembers her. Her e-mails. She will be there in a month. They will both be there. Without spouses. Hers because he's afraid to fly, and his because she has to stay home and take care of Chelsea. "She'll be old enough to stay with your folks in a few more years," he assured his wife. "And, it's not like you're missing anything."

The company's annual banquet in Vegas. The awards banquet. The annual rendezvous. This year they decided to save money and just stay in the same room. "We'll make love in the morning," she wrote in a recent e-mail. They booked a hotel other than the conference hotel. "We'll pretend we're married," she wrote. For the last month she has e-mailed every other day. She called the house once. He told her not to anymore. Her e-mail had been down for a few days, she explained. She said that she needed to call just to make sure of something. She hung up before she said what. He'd known her in college because they took many of the same business classes together.

The car. The muffler. He thinks he hears it, but knows that he can't. There are no roads near the path. Farmland and woods. That's it. In another half mile the path crosses a county road, but that's another half mile. If he makes it to that road and then turns around and makes it home, he'll have gone six miles. Six miles, he thinks. Farther than I've ever gone.

Two years ago they recognized each other. They sat together through the awards. They clicked. "I don't love him anymore," she said. He did not tell her the same. I love my wife. I love my daughter. Last year he told her that it was over. They couldn't do it anymore. But then she e-mailed.

Once a year, he thinks. Something to help me get through everything else. Fifty to sixty hours a week making the idiots above me look good. He shakes his head. If anything, seeing her once a year makes me a better husband. He imagines his wife and daughter. He will look in on Chelsea when he gets home, the warm pocket she becomes in sleep. Sliding in next to her, he will put his arm around his wife. He will sleep that way as long as he can because that's what she likes. He will try not to roll away.

At the county road, he bends over with his hands on his knees. The bad one hurts. I stopped too many times. I went too far. The cold catches up with him, and he shivers. He looks to his left. South. The road stretches off and disappears into the blackness. The light here is distant—small specks that must be the windows of farmhouses miles away. Lit windows. He counts how many days before he will see her. Less than a month.

The engine starts, and the muffler growls into the silence.

He jumps, and adrenaline churns through him. Headlight washes over him from his right. He stands upright, shields the light with his hand. A single headlamp and the grumbling muffler. His heart thumps against his ribs, echoes in his ears.

"Thought you might make it out this far tonight," a voice calls from behind the light. It's a deep voice, like his own. "Your face just said that tonight you might make it."

"What? I don't..." He steps back.

"This is farther than you've ever come before."

He glares through his fingers towards what he guesses is the windshield. He squints and waits. "And that's important to you for some reason, asshole?"

For a moment the muffler drones. "Now, don't get angry. We're both night owls, right? We're both hunters. We know why we're out here."

The car is fifteen feet away. He looks down the path. If I hear the car door ... if the door makes the slightest fucking creak, I'm gone. He guesses he can out sprint him. "You've got nothing better to do? You sit here and wait for people to come down the bike path? You like scaring people?"

"I don't wait for people," the driver calls. "I was waiting for you. I thought you might make it out this far tonight. You've usually turned around by now."

He steps down the path. He stops at the edge of the light.

"You can't run away," the driver calls.

"Do you think this is fucking scaring me? Do you think I'd have a hard time describing your car to the cops?" He looks hard, but the car is all headlight and muffler noise. And, around it, blackness.

The driver is quiet.

"Just get out if that's what you're going to do, mother fucker. Just do what you're going to do..." He catches his own yelling. He looks down the path again. It's a gray strip through the darker blackness. His eyes have adjusted. He'll have that advantage if it comes down to a chase.

"What I'm going to do?"

He takes another step away from the car.

"Do you think I'm going to hurt you? Do you think there's anything I can do to you? To you?" The driver's question hangs in the air and is soon followed by laughter.

Something feels wrong, gone bad. "I don't know what..."

The car's transmission shifts, thunks into a gear.

"Tell me one thing. Do you still keep it there?" the driver asks.

"Keep it?" He feels dizzy. "What are you..."

"The key. Do you still keep the key under the left front tire of your car?"

He tries to swallow. Chelsea. His wife ... his girls. His girls at home. "No," he says. "No. Don't you..."

The car starts to roll backwards. "You're too far out," the driver calls. "You're going to lose them."

"No!" He runs at the car, but it rockets backward down the shoulder. The gravel shooting up from under the tires stings him, gets in his eyes. He stops. Half a football field away, the car slows, pulls a u-turn across the road, and flips to nothing but taillights. They shrink into the distance, like eyes sinking back into a cave. The muffler roars.

He stops. He runs to the path—the only sure way he knows back to his house. He can hear the muffler, loud, growling into the distance. There is no light here. He runs as fast as he can. No, he thinks. No. No. No. His knee twinges, twinges, twinges. Something finally gives, blows out. He goes down.

Self-Defense

Picture it in detail. Fantasize if necessary.

They do.

3:49 p.m. Acting out the motion of putting her key in the ignition, Samantha closes her eyes and leans back against the leather seat. She tries to take a smooth, deep breath, but the air comes in staccato. She exhales slowly, calming herself.

Make fear. Then, fight through it. Imagine doing exactly what needs to be done.

Samantha's pulse is insistent in her wrists, behind her ears ... her heart pistons in her chest.

His arm slips suddenly around her throat, pinching her windpipe shut.

Act immediately. Visualize constantly until the reaction becomes instinct.

Samantha loads her arm forward and then launches her elbow over the back seat fifteen times in rapid succession.

This is life or death.

The hard bone of her joint meets his ear, his temple, his cheek. He turns his head, and her elbow breaks his nose. Her ambition is to drive it straight back into his skull.

Highly trained people—even black belts—freeze in the face of sudden violence. They aren't prepared mentally. They haven't envisioned the worst.

The attacker plays it over in his mind again and again and again. He lives it to the point that the actual thing feels more like a dream, like something he's watching. It's easy, then.

The arm disappears from around her throat to grasp at the pain she has caused. Samantha grabs her door handle, pulls it up, explodes from the car.

Don't forget. Earsplitting noise is an excellent ally.

She opens her mouth as though to scream. Her jaw pops, but she is silent. She doesn't want to startle anyone who might be in the parking garage. It's only supposed to be a visualization.

She checks under the car again. Another driver shoots past her. Listening to its hollow echo, she sees the car in her mind turning corners downwards towards the exit. The pay booth is vacant. Everything is automated.

She gets back into her empty car and sits behind the wheel. What if the arm had stayed? What if the elbowing to the face hadn't been enough?

Never underestimate the pain threshold of an attacker. He is full of adrenaline. And rage.

Samantha shuts her eyes.

His arm still constricts her against her seat like a bungee cord.

Fingernails. Teeth. Both are good and inexpensive weapons.

Samantha sees herself injecting her nails into his forearm until his grip loosens. She moves her head until her incisors find skin and muscle and fat. She bites with the goal of having a piece of his flesh pull away from his bone into her mouth. Then, released, she would bolt again.

Always run. Towards light. Towards voices. Towards people. Run. And scream.

She turns her engine over. She doesn't shift into *Drive*. Pressing the button, she locks all of her doors. They are already locked, but she is reassured by the stereo sound of the thunk.

She's exhausted by what she's imagined. Like sound delayed after a flash of lightning, her fear now crackles inside her. She can't move.

Her instructor is going to attack her in the next three days. It's her final test. So far, he's had the morning and early afternoon. So far, nothing. She learned at three o'clock that she needs to catch an eleven-thirty flight for Bangladesh. There are difficulties on site that need face-to-face attention. She's decided not to tell her instructor about her departure.

5:16 p.m. Samantha's little Lhasa Apso, Honey, strains at its leash, pulling ahead, running into yards. Samantha carries her cell phone in her other hand. Her son, Kevin, walks along beside her. She looks over her shoulder. Would he attack her while she's with her son?

Expect it at any time. Never feel safe. Women are attacked in busy department store parking lots. Women are raped in churches or elementary school lavatories. Those who want to do harm have often planned it weeks or even months in advance. He watches for a long time, waiting for places where his victim won't be careful.

The thin wires that dangle from each of Kevin's ears meet below his throat and disappear into his jacket. He's always plugged into his music.

"Will you be all right while I'm gone?" Samantha asks.

Kevin stares blankly ahead, seeming to study something only he can see.

"Hey." Samantha pulls his sleeve.

He reaches up and pops the tiny speaker out of his right ear. "Yeah?"

She repeats her question.

He shrugs. "It ain't the first time I've been alone. You were gone for six days last time." His hand moves to restore the music.

"Isn't," Samantha corrects.

"What?"

She shakes her head. "You weren't alone. Grandma's right across town."

He looks at her. "You brought it up. I don't mind being by myself. I don't need Grandma."

Honey stops abruptly on a front lawn. Circles and sniffs.

Kevin starts to say something.

She stops him, points at Honey. "She's doing her business." Samantha looks around, but nobody is in the neighborhood. She studies bushes, behind trees, under porches.

Someone could be anywhere.

Honey finds something in the grass and sniffs it joyously. Her tail swishes.

"Honey, don't!" Samantha yanks the leash, pulling the dog from the feces left by another dog. Honey lurches to the side, making a half-yelping, half-choking sound. Her front nails scratch back onto the sidewalk.

"Mom, you're hurting her!"

Samantha pulls the dog along a little faster. Honey walks obediently at her heel, looks back once. "Ugh, I hate that," she says. "It makes me nauseous."

"Why? She's not using your nose. It's natural—"

Samantha's cell phone vibrates in her hand. She holds up a halting finger to Kevin. "Just one minute." She opens it and reads. Two emails. One is from the airline. The flight has been delayed by an hour and fifteen minutes.

In her side view, Kevin adjusts his earphones, tunes out.

The second email is from the office. RE: Go Get 'Em, Sam. It explains the problem with the Bangladeshi engineers and the aspects of the project to which they are opposed. Convince them otherwise is the gist of the message. Remind them that the operation would be easier in a place without monsoons. Remind them of the money the project brings into their country. Remind them about who is in charge. Keep this thing moving.

Samantha closes her cell phone and looks at Kevin. She had invited him to walk the dog with her. He had said yes. Something in his fifteen-year-old face had reminded her of the five-year-old he used to be. She wants to say something to him. Touch his shoulder. Something.

He reaches into his pocket, flips open his phone, and starts typing feverishly with his thumbs. He waits a second, chuckles, and then types more.

Samantha opens her own phone and replies to the email. She lets the project manager know that she is in charge and is going to show Bangladesh that American women have balls. She smiles to herself, imagining Dave receiving the message. He will laugh.

Ahead, an old man in baggy trousers stands in his front yard watering his lawn. He lives ten houses from Samantha's. She doesn't know him. Doesn't know his wife or if he even has a wife.

Everyone could be an attacker, even neighbors. Especially neighbors. They watch routines. They know.

Samantha looks at the man and feels him pressing his weight down onto her, pushing her back into the wet lawn. She imagines grabbing into the crotch of his trousers, finding testicles. She feels them in her hand and crushes them like two hard-boiled egg yolks. Squeeze, twist, and pull.

The technique can drop a giant.

She draws back at Kevin's touch. "You all right, Mom?"

"Fine."

8:02 p.m. Samantha lies in her dark bedroom. Somewhere in the groggy tossing and turning she must have slept. Her mind goes again to her ex-husband. She'd been in China the last time she saw Jason a year and a half ago.

"Libby?" So odd to hear her name on a busy street in the city of Chongqing. It wasn't really her name, just a nickname left over from childhood ... the name Jason always used for her. She'd never told him that she hated it.

They ate hotpot. They drank Chongqing beer and green tea with whiskey. They danced disco at Babi. She knew about his fiancé, a woman from Finland. She didn't care. They had sex as they had once had sex in the easy, earliest days.

Thinking of it, she rubs her legs against each other and then finally throw off the sheets and gets up. She's been with nobody since.

Be careful when dating. Most women are attacked by men that they've invited into their lives.

She wouldn't see Jason in Asia. Even if she tried, even if she wanted, his company had long since moved him and Sylvi to South Africa. Sylvi is pregnant. When he calls to talk to Kevin, he doesn't call her Libby anymore. He calls her Samantha, and she knows that every fragment of what they once had is gone. She'd asked for the divorce. She remembers that at one time she'd had a list of reasons.

8:49 p.m. Standing in the kitchen, Samantha calls his name, but she knows already that Kevin isn't home. She is alone in the house. She checks the front door. It's always locked. They never use it. Garage door. Unlocked. Patio door. Unlocked.

The walls of her mouth dry. Would he go as far as to sneak into her home while she slept? Was he that dedicated in his teaching?

Intruders are dedicated. They are addicted to the rush of attacking others. Women are often attacked in their own homes. They feel the most safe. They are the most vulnerable.

Samantha breathes in through her nose, out through her mouth. She takes a deep breath while pushing out her stomach muscles. She holds the breath to a count of three as she's been taught. She exhales, pulls in her stomach, and repeats the word *Calm* in her mind. Opening the closet, she finds the small steel box. Inside is Kevin's birth certificate, his swaddling cloth from the hospital, her BS in Engineering, her MBA, and her silvery Ladysmith .357 magnum. She picks it up and hefts its loaded weight.

"I have a gun," Samantha says, raising her voice into the basement. She turns on every light. She flashlights behind the furnace, the water heater, into the closet with the breaker box. She aims the gun in front of her. Honey follows her dutifully. Upstairs, she checks the crawl space off of the guest room. She checks under beds. After twenty minutes, she is convinced that she is alone.

9:32 p.m. She fishes a macaroni and cheese box from the garbage and places it into the recycling bin. A pot on the stove is stained orange and crusted with dehydrated noodles. She shakes her head, picks up her cell phone, and presses a button.

She gets his voicemail. She hangs up. She calls back a moment later. "Geez, Kevin, thanks for leaving the house wide open when you left. Oh, and thanks for the mess in the kitchen." She snaps her phone shut.

She stares at the window. The light inside and the dark outside turn the glass into a mirror. Concentrating, she sees beyond her pale reflection. Silhouettes of trees. Dim lights coming from neighboring houses. Mostly it's darkness.

He could be out there. Waiting. He wants to test her.

10:12 p.m. She has learned to travel light. Everything is reduced down to one carry-on and her laptop. Emptying the contents of her bag onto the bed, she packs it again, checking each item against her travel checklist.

The bag and the laptop case side by side on the bed make her melancholy. She is leaving. She will be gone for days. Kevin will be home. She has nobody else.

She opens her cell phone and calls him.

"The subscriber you are trying to reach is unavailable."

The tears come, as they do more often now. She pushes them away with her fingertips. Shaking her head, she chuckles disparagingly at herself. "You're being pathetic, Samantha," she whispers.

She puts Honey in her crate, hoping Kevin will be home soon to let her out. He could be anywhere. She's met few of his friends.

Backing out into the street, she realizes that she took no precautions in the garage. She didn't check her surroundings, didn't check under the car, didn't check the backseat. Pulling up to the curb, she turns on the dome light and looks into the back. Nothing. She turns around and shifts into *Drive*.

It takes one slip-up. Too optimistic, become a statistic. He chuckled. I have that one copyrighted in case I ever write a book.

She drives and tries to remember what she can of the Bangladeshi customs she reviewed. Accept all invitations to dinner. Eat with fingers. Showing emotion in business is considered rude. Do everything with the right hand. The left hand is unclean. Businesswomen in Bangladesh don't shake hands, but nod their heads politely.

Even as she rehearses the etiquette, she can't keep images of violence out of her mind. A Bangladeshi man, posing as room service, raping her in her room. A man pulling her into the dark alleys of Dhaka. The engineers closing the door to the meeting room, locking it, and making her know her place.

The highway is speckled here and there with taillights. It haunts her how easily she forgot to be cautious. He could have been in her garage. Anyone could. She checks her rearview mirror. How long has that set of headlights been behind her?

Attackers might follow potential victims for months—discerning patterns, looking for weaknesses, gauging vulnerability.

She opens her phone to call Kevin. She has three emails waiting. They are reminders from work of upcoming meetings—meetings she won't be able to attend because she will be in Bangladesh. She reads them, looking from the tiny screen to the road and back to the screen.

She remembers the rearview mirror. The headlights.

All the lights behind her look the same, like pairs of flashlights trying to find her.

11:17 p.m. She pulls into long-term parking and finds a spot. Getting out, she is surrounded by acres of cars. She takes her laptop around to her trunk to get her carry-on. She scans for the airport shuttle. A breeze of cigarette odor blows over her. Reaching into the darkness, she finds the strap and starts to loop it around her arm to bring it up to her shoulder. Then, she hears footsteps approaching her from behind. She freezes.

How could it be him? How could he know? He couldn't.

I could be anywhere. It will be just like a real attack. That's the point of the test.

He didn't know that she was leaving the country.

The five most hazardous words in self-defense. "It won't happen to me." Everybody thinks it. Still, it happens to people who probably thought it would never happen to them. They weren't ready.

The footsteps are getting closer. She takes a long breath, pictures herself doing what she needs to do.

Fight. I have protection where I need it. I've done this with over one hundred women. Just concentrate on what needs to be done. Don't let me win.

Samantha swallows, listening. Timing it. It might not even be him.

It might be someone worse.

A laptop case is lined with steel. Add the weight of the computer, it's like carrying around a size 24 steel-toed boot. Use it.

Samantha spins with the force of a discus thrower. The laptop case connects with someone's head. A body hits the ground. It doesn't move.

11:22 p.m. Samantha runs toward the dim light of the parking attendant's kiosk nearly a quarter of a mile away. She's screaming.

Insomnia

Across the street, the two shadows, darker than the gray dark around them, stagger away from the sidewalk and up the neighbor's porch steps.

"I can feel my heart," Luke whispers. He sits next to Gordon on the couch. They are in the darkness of their house watching the darkness of the neighborhood.

Gordon shushes him.

"They can't hear us, Dad."

"Maybe they can."

A car slows for the stop sign at the cross street. Its taillights flare red, and then it turns out of sight.

"They took the newspaper," Luke says.

Gordon squints at the two men moving on the sidewalk. Each has the small orange ember of a cigarette between his fingers. The taller of the two holds the pale, fat roll of the Sunday edition in his hand. "Paperboy comes too early," Gordon says. "Why can't he wait until the morning like other paperboys?"

"Maybe he can't sleep," Luke says. "Like us." He gets up and goes to the window. "I'm going to knock on the glass."

"No." Gordon guesses that the men are stumbling home from one of the nearby bars.

Luke looks at the floor.

Knocking on the glass. What would it do? Nothing. It would only call attention to their house, which had yet to fall victim to the random acts of unkindness associated with the night's endless foot traffic. "Just close the curtains," Gordon says, "I'll turn on television." He opens his laptop and its dim light glows back into the room.

Luke sits on the couch. "Sorry, Dad."

"Look, don't ... you're right." Gordon rubs his eyes. "It's just that knocking on the window won't do anything."

The boy nods, drifting off into a cartoon.

Gordon watches him. "You should read, or I should give you some worksheets."

"Dad, it's summer."

Gordon smiles, nodding. "The new t-shirt is up on the site. Want to see it?"

Luke leans over toward the screen, which shows both views of the shirt. The front reads, TUBIN' OR NOT TUBIN'? The back reads, THAT'S A QUESTION?

Gordon had found a website that produced, marketed, and sold t-shirts. He only needed to send in the words. A year ago, on a whim, he'd sent in an idea for a black t-shirt with white lettering that read, HOME'S COOLER. After about two months, mothers of home-schooled kids found out about the shirt and it, according to the site administrators, produced record sales. Gordon spent his time trying to come up with other slogans. He had twenty-six on the site but only a few—like I'M ALLERGIC TO PEOPLE and I JAM THEREFORE I AM (which was popular with musicians and those who put up their own preserves) saw any kind of significant sales. Even so, he liked the idea of making money from home.

"Who's this for?" Luke asks, tapping his finger on the screen.

"Tubers."

"Tubers?"

Gordon explains that there are people who like to be pulled on gigantic inner tubes behind speedboats. "Your mother and I used to do it ... before you were born."

Luke looks at him wide-eyed. "You weren't afraid?"

"We were young."

Luke looks out the window.

"I didn't know anything about loss," Gordon says. He wonders if his son would believe him if he told him that he had spent one summer in college as a bouncer. The bar wasn't a very rough place, and his main job was to clean up at the end of the night. Still, he did confront his share of rowdy drunks, and even tossed a few out. Such memories lodged in his head feel as though they belong to somebody else.

Luke sets his hand in his father's hands. Gordon relishes the small warmth of it. He closes his laptop and watches the cartoon, feeling how easy it is to get lost in such a thing.

"Did Mom ever tell you about Sam Harrington?" Luke asks during one of the commercials.

Gordon thinks about it and shakes his head.

"He helped people that nobody else would help. Mom told me about him a few times when she'd put me to bed. She said he was important."

"You remember that?"

"Kind of," Luke says.

Even with her own young son at home, Sheila never stopped volunteering at the women's shelter. A man came one evening with a bag full of donations. When Sheila buzzed him in, he grabbed her neck, cracked her head against the security glass, and ran down the hallway looking for his battered wife's room. His actions, which he most likely blamed on love or heartache, had killed Sheila.

"Mom wasn't always careful," Gordon says. He squeezes Luke's hand. The autumn after Sheila's death, Gordon pulled Luke out of public school for the safety of home schooling.

"But she was a good person," Luke says.

"She was a good person."

"She wouldn't have liked those men."

The men had come other nights, talking loudly as though they were still trying to hear each other over the noise of a juke box. Restless, they shoved each other. Sometimes they trampled wild flowers in front yards. Other times they knocked over real estate signs. Gordon had known men like them. They always behaved themselves in the bars, not wanting to risk being cut off. Their anger was for outside.

Inside is always the safest place.

"Nobody would like those men," Gordon says.

Luke brings his hand back into his own lap. "She would have done something."

At Luke's request, Gordon had called the police a few times to report the vandalism or petty thieveries. When the police cruiser would finally drive down the street, the men would be long since gone. Gordon called on a fourth occasion. The dispatcher said they'd do what they could, which turned out to be nothing. "They didn't even send a car this time," Luke said, looking out the window into the gloaming. He never mentioned the police again.

"Come on," Gordon says, "let's just get ready for bed. We need to try to get up for the Tigers game. They're playing at one."

Later in the week, a thump against the porch floor, followed by staccato footsteps down the porch steps, wakes Gordon fully from a drifting half-sleep. He guesses that his online grocery order has arrived.

It's three o'clock in the afternoon. Noises come to him through his closed window. He sits up, realizing that it's the neighbor's children across the street riding their bikes in their driveway. He watches them go around and around the small space. When the little girl falls, her older brother stops riding, rubs her elbow, and helps her back on her bike. They seem like nice kids. Still, they are too close to the road, too close to the sidewalk, too much in the shadow of that old elm that might fall, too exposed to the dogs that could be roaming the neighborhood. Gordon turns away from their helpless exposure.

Luke is awake, unpacking the grocery box.

Gordon makes coffee. "I told you not to open the front door."

Luke's hand hovers holding a package of spaghetti noodles. "It was just to pull the box in. I didn't go out on the porch."

Gordon looks at him until the boy meets his eye. "Don't open the front door."

"Okay. Fine."

Gordon sits, watching the browned water drip down into the pot. The smell of coffee blooms into the room. He enjoys the warming realization that he can soon check his email for more sales.

Luke puts the dry goods away. The perishables won't come until their scheduled time on Friday.

"Do you think they'll do it again?" he asks.

"What?"

He breaks down the empty box. "Those men. Do you think they'll steal the neighbor's paper again?"

Gordon looks at him. "How would I know? Why are you even thinking about them?"

Luke shrugs. "When I opened the door, I saw today's paper on the neighbor's porch. I saw the kids riding bikes."

"It's bugging you, huh?"

Luke nods.

"Maybe we can do something," Gordon says, picking up the phone. He calls the newspaper office and after one transfer is speaking to the circulation manager. He explains about the paperboy and the stolen paper.

"Coming too early? That's a new one."

As they speak, it comes up that Gordon isn't a subscriber. The circulation manager asks him if he's interested in becoming one.

"No, I hate newspapers."

The circulation manager says he'll see what he can do about the paperboy coming too early.

Gordon hangs up and looks at Luke.

"Dad, you should have said that you're not interested in subscribing if it means your paper is going to get stolen every weekend."

He studies the boy.

The next weekend the paperboy comes as early as ever. Gordon checks his t-shirt sales. It's been a bad week. Luke kneels in front of the window.

Gordon closes his laptop. "Come away from there. Why don't you read or—"

"Shh. They're back."

Gordon scrabbles his hand around the couch cushion for the remote and shuts off the television.

"They took the paper again." Luke's voice is heavy with defeat.

Gordon leans back into the couch. "Well, we tried. I doubt that the circulation manager even—"

"They're peeing!"

"What?" Gordon stands and leans toward the window. The two men are in the neighbor's front yard with their backs to Gordon's house, standing with their legs spread as though they're being frisked. Two luminescent streams start at their crotches and end on the lawn. The taller of the two has the newspaper pinched between his arm and his ribs. They relieve themselves for nearly a minute. Gordon has seen the neighbor's children sitting in the grass exactly where the puddles of urine are forming.

"Dad, why would they do that? Why do they hate those people?"

"They don't hate them. It's just..." Gordon feels the weight of the questions he can't really answer. Why are adults like this? Why aren't they better to each other? Why does everything seem like a random mess, ungoverned by any god that is judicious or caring?

As though watching himself do it, Gordon raps his fist against the window three times. Before the men can turn, he pulls Luke to the kitchen. Crouching in the breakfast nook, he waits for the sound of his front door being kicked in.

"That was stupid of me."

"They're probably gone, Dad," Luke says after a minute.

Gordon isn't sure. A faint pulse beats in his knuckles where they met the glass, matching the rhythm of his heart hammering against his ribs.

"I think you were right, anyway," Luke says, standing. "Knocking on the glass doesn't do anything."

Gordon has never met the neighbor. He goes to the city's official website and types in the neighbor's address for a property tax query. It turns up their names: Wallace, Connor F. & Jennifer. It's four o'clock in the morning. Gordon writes down the name and then looks it up in the phone book that was recently left on his porch. It's three o'clock the next day when he dials.

Luke stands near him, smiling. "Tell him that he needs one of those motion lights," he whispers. "I saw them on TV."

"Shh. It's ringing."

Someone picks up on the other end. Gordon asks for Connor.

"You got him."

Whatever words he had imagined himself saying have left him.

"Dad..."

"I don't buy anything over the phone, buddy," Connor Wallace says. "Is that what you're trying to do? Sell me something?"

Luke pulls at his hand. "Tell him that you're his neighbor. Tell him."

Gordon stands for a moment with the heaviness of the phone in his hand. "I watch your house," he says.

"What?"

He feels like he's stumbling through an impromptu speech in high school. He can't stop. "At night. I watch your house at night. I've seen—"

The connection goes to dial tone.

Gordon stares at the phone as though it were a dead bird that he'd suddenly found in his hand. He looks down at Luke. "He hung up."

"You probably freaked him out. 'I watch your house.'? That sounds psycho, Dad. You have to call him back. Tell him that you're his neighbor. Tell him—"

"Okay. I'll call him back." He punches in the number again. "Don't hang up," he says to the dead air he encounters on the other end. "I just wanted to say—"

"What did you want to say, Gordon LaFarge?"

He goes silent at the sound of his full name in the other man's mouth.

"That's right. I have your name right fucking here. Why don't you learn to block your number before you make prank calls, pervert? Maybe I should look you up in the phone book, drive over, and beat the sh—"

Gordon slams down the phone. His mouth tingles as though he might vomit. "That's it," he says to Luke, to his wife, to a part of himself that won't keep quiet. "That's it. We're done. No more. We're done."

That night he orders blinds fitted for the front window and installs them when they arrive two days later. What they know of the neighborhood anymore is the doppling hum of passing cars and the muted conversations of those walking by. Gordon lets Luke watch television every night until morning.

His tubing t-shirt does well. As it turns out, there are also people who float down rivers on inflated tubes. Hundreds of businesses along hundreds of rivers rent tubes out so thousands of people can spend an afternoon floating. Many of these rental places want to have Gordon's latest t-shirt in stock. He watches his online account swell with deposits. He checks his email every half hour. The summer nights soon blend one into the next.

Sometimes he imagines himself floating helplessly, half-naked, surrounded by others on tubes. He expects the idea to always leave him nauseous, though sometimes he catches himself with a dreamy half-smile on his face.

It's several nights later at three thirty in the morning when someone's determined knocking booms from the front door. Reflexively, Gordon presses off the television and pulls Luke closer to him. They sit in the darkness, listening.

The knocking hammers again.

"Dad, you—"

"Shh."

The doorbell rings. Luke stands too quickly for Gordon to pull him back into his grip.

The dark shadow of his son stands five feet from him, like a haunting. "I'm going to get it if you don't, Dad."

"Luke, sit down," he hisses.

There's more frantic knocking.

"Coming!" Luke hollers, not moving.

The man on the other side of the door shouts.

Gordon knows that Luke is studying his hunched silhouette cowering on the couch. He stands. He breathes deeply and steps to the foyer. The dark outline of a head moves on the other side of the door's small window. "Who is it?" Gordon says.

"Your neighbor. You've got a fire!"

Gordon does nothing, guessing that it's a trick. That's the kind of line criminals use to get fools to open their doors.

Luke reaches past him and turns on the front light. "Dad!" The boy turns the deadbolt and opens the door to a tall, blonde man squinting in the sudden brightness. It's Connor

Wallace, the neighbor from across the street. He cradles a fire extinguisher the color of a heart.

"Where's your basement?!"

Gordon's mouth moves. Nothing comes out.

"I think your house is on fire! Where's your basement?"

Gordon feels weighted by this news. His adrenaline doesn't spread to his limbs but instead seems to back up into his head, leaving a deafening roar.

"Follow me," Luke says. "Come on."

The man pushes past Gordon, and Luke leads him through the dark to the back of the house.

The smell of the smoke drifts to the foyer. He hears his son calling down to the basement. "Don't you go down those stairs, Luke," Gordon manages to shout. A fire engine pulls up along the street—all lights and men and radio dispatch squawk. Three shadows run toward the house.

The firemen double check to make certain that the fire is out. Connor Wallace paces an excited circle. "I'm pretty sure I got it all," he says. The firemen take down Gordon's name and insurance information. Gordon eyes him, but Connor doesn't react when he hears Gordon's full name spoken aloud. He's talking to one of the firemen. "Lot of juice in these babies," he says, holding up his extinguisher. "Lot of juice."

The firemen seem almost seven feet tall in their uniforms and with their questions. While they are there, the house belongs to them, and they move about freely. Luke follows them around as though he's been called to a new religion.

The battalion chief turns to Connor Wallace to get his story. He explains that he had a few beers before bed and then woke in the middle of the night to use the bathroom. He opens Gordon's blind and points to his house and shows them the bathroom window.

"I saw what looked like a wisp of smoke coming from the foundation of his house," he says, and moves his hand. He guessed that he was just seeing things. Then, while flushing, he took another look, and the smoke was heavier. "I called you guys on my cell and then ran over here with this little baby."

The battalion chief and the other firemen commend Connor. The chief turns back to Gordon. "Just check that vent about once every three months. It's just a little thing, but it can be huge. Lots of houses have burned to the ground because of a dryer fire."

Gordon nods. Standing, he follows Luke who follows the other men to the door.

Connor walks with one of the fireman towards the truck. "I mean, at first I didn't think it was anything. Next thing you know I'm in some basement putting out a fire."

Gordon goes back to the couch. His guilt and fear and shame settle over him like heavy clothes pulling him down into a drowning. He drifts in his numbness and is startled when Luke turns off the television.

"I think I'm going to go to bed."

Gordon looks at the darkness outside. "Already?"

"I'm just tired," he says. "I think most people sleep at night." He stops with his foot on the first step to the upstairs. "You didn't even thank him, Dad."

"What?"

"That man who put out the fire. Mr. Wallace. You didn't even say thank you."

"That's right, I didn't," he murmurs. "What's wrong with me?"

"I don't know," Luke says, disappearing up the stairs.

A few days later, the doorbell rings at two in the afternoon. Gordon opens his eyes. He'd heard a lawnmower earlier, and he guesses that the guy from the lawn service is at the door to collect his check. The man is shy, and their exchanges are always mercifully brief. He gets out of bed and pulls on pants.

He opens his front door to Connor Wallace's broad grin. The neighbor leans up against a large box. "I almost left," Connor says, patting his hand on the cardboard. "I saw them deliver this baby about an hour ago. New dryer, huh?" He looks at Gordon for a moment. "What, you sleeping in?"

Gordon shrugs.

"Sometimes my wife lets me do that on a Sunday—just sleep and sleep." He smiles at Gordon and pats the box again.

"Let's say we tear this thing out of the box and put it in your basement."

Footsteps come down the stairs behind Gordon. He turns and sees Luke on the landing. The boy comes and stands by his side.

He puts his hand on top of Luke's head. "This is Luke, my son."

"I remember." Connor holds out his hand and Luke shakes it. "He was my man with the plan. Shouted down to me how to work the fire extinguisher."

Gordon looks at his son.

Luke smiles. "They showed us in school once."

Connor tries to break his fingers into the cardboard. The staples won't give. "You got a utility knife? We'll get a better grip on it if we get it out of the box."

Gordon studies him. "Why do you want to help?"

Connor stands for a moment and then smiles. "To help, I guess."

Luke pulls on Gordon's arm and whispers in his ear when he leans down to him. "He's like Sam Harrington, Dad. Good Sam Harrington."

While they carry the dryer to the basement and haul the old, blackened one out, Connor retells the story of the fire. "I still can't believe it," he says. "Sometimes you surprise yourself."

Gordon listens to him.

Luke's internal clock shifts slowly through August. Most nights he is still up until two in the morning. He's awake on a Saturday night when the men come again. Gordon left the blind where it was ever since Connor had opened it the night of the fire.

"They're back, Dad."

Gordon closes his laptop. "They're back, huh?" He leans toward the window. One of the men is trying to balance himself on Connor's little girl's bicycle. He gets his feet on the pedals and, with knees pumping into his chest, he rides around in a shaky circle. The other man laughs. Gordon hears it faintly.

"He's too big for that bike," Luke says. "He'll break it."

Gordon pushes himself up from the couch and stands. "Alright," he says, "Sonuvabitch, alright." He starts for the door.

"Where are you going, Dad?"

Gordon tells him to call the police. "Tell them that there's an assault happening near the corner of Fifth and Kennedy."

"Dad, what's an assault? Dad—"

"Luke, just call 911 now. Just tell them what I told you."

He opens the door. The night air is warm and thick and swells his pores. The neighborhood hums around him with air conditioners. His heart is a trapped animal in his chest. "Hey," he calls, coming down his porch stairs. Both men are much bigger than him.

They look his way. The bigger of the two stands and lets the bicycle fall over between his legs.

Gordon winces at the idea of their hitting him. They will hit him. They're drunk enough that they might even kick him once he's down. He swallows and starts to cross the street. "What do you think you're doing?"

"Kicking your ass in about ten seconds," the bigger one says after a moment.

Gordon knows it's true. He keeps walking. If the police arrive in time, there'll be trouble enough for the two of them. Maybe even some jail time. Something.

Reaching the other side of the street where the men are raising their fists, Gordon senses that one way or another, he will be able to sleep tonight.

Sleeping Deeply

After Julia Pomaville's dinner party, Bruce Hunter quietly battled a bout of insomnia, which led to him discovering a man in his basement. He blamed his sleeplessness on Julia. Just as the merlot started to give him a slight buzz, she'd started reading a "heart-breaking and sublime" letter from a soldier. She'd found it stuck in the pages of a book she'd bought at a used bookstore. Gathered around her on over-stuffed furniture, her dinner guests listened. After a few sentences, nobody sipped their wine.

"I wish I could lie to you, Dad," Julia read. "I wish I could tell you that I'm coping. You asked if I'm keeping focused on the idea of coming home. Honestly, I don't think I can come home ... even if I get there. Home is dead for me. Everything is dead." Julia cleared her throat.

"Yesterday I found a kid's arm. I couldn't tell if it had belonged to a little boy or a little girl. I walked around with that arm—trying to feel something. Anything. I couldn't. I pried open the little fist and found a quarter. I kept it. I thought I should keep it—you know, make it mean something. Later, I threw the quarter away. That's the kind of man I am now. Nothing means shit to me. I'm a stone.

"Stones don't go home. Stones are just stones. They stay the same. Hard. Cold. Dead. Doesn't matter where they are. You can't imagine what it feels like to live this way. Me? I can't imagine people with happy lives. I know too much about the sadness beneath happiness. The people here—they beg from us every day. I have nothing to give them.

"I don't want to come home. I don't want to stay here. I don't want to die, but I really don't want all that much to live.

You asked in your letter how I'm doing, Dad. I just didn't want to lie. I hope Christmas is good. I'll bet it's tough without Mom."

Wendy, Bruce's very pregnant wife, wiped tears from her eyes. Then, her hands went back to the business of rubbing her belly like a crystal ball. The party broke up shortly after the reading of the letter.

Wendy's old black-and-white sit-coms put her out soon after they went to bed. At least she was finally getting some sleep. Her back had been keeping her awake for the past couple of weeks. Bruce muted the sound, letting the dim light flicker silently in the room. *On the Water Front*. The priest had the dock workers in the basement of the church. He was trying to get them to take a stand for the good of the group.

The soldier's words repeated in Bruce's head. What he was feeling reminded him of what he felt the one time he borrowed the neighbor's canoe and took it out onto Lake Missaukee, where they had their summer cottage. The canoe had struck him as novel, even adventurous. It would be something different from the speedboat. For the past five years, he'd been haunted by a restlessness and the notion that if he tried different things, his life might feel more alive.

Wendy had laughed at him from the dock.

Floating in the motionless canoe, he held up one hand. "How."

She shook her head, laughing again.

Paddling, he was drawn into coves and inlets, finding gloomy scenes that seemed out of place on their spring-fed vacation lake. The water was black, and each stroke swirled up an eddy of sewage-sweet muck. Tree stumps, jagged and weathered gray, stuck up from the water like ruins. Prehistoric snapping turtles slid from logs or lifted their long necks to watch him. It was in these hidden bays that the trash of the lake ended up ... Styrofoam cups, glass and plastic bottles, butane lighters, Ziploc, grocery, and chip bags, beer cans, cigarette wrappers, popsicle sticks, old bobbers, worm containers, chewing tobacco tins, half-deflated beach balls, and the rotting pieces of old docks and diving floats.

Gliding across the surface of these hidden pockets of water with nothing to hear but the sound of lily pads rubbing hauntingly against the underside of the canoe, Bruce felt uneasy

... like the uneasiness he felt when the soldier's descriptions replayed in his mind.

Why did she have to read that damn letter?

An unfamiliar noise creaked in the basement. A window on its hinges? Bruce thought for a moment and then pushed down the covers and got out of bed, making certain not to wake Wendy. He looked at the clock. 2:16.

He'd been on edge for nearly a month. Five weeks of vacation. It was the most time he'd ever taken off. It was his compromise to Wendy ... time around the house before her due date. She had hoped for him to be home just after the birth, but that was the time that he would be in Denver. Saved vacation or no, he had to go. He'd overseen the demographic studies. He understood and could present the nuances of the reports. There were rumors of a promotion if he could pull this off. A seventh Denver-based discount department store to break ground in one of the city's older suburbs. Some local officials were opposed. They had arguments about what it might do to small businesses in the area. Bruce's job was to convince them otherwise.

He thought preparations would keep him busy. Instead, he finished the nursery in three days. There was little else to do but wait. What the time off gave him more than anything was too much thinking. A vague darkness caught up to him—a darkness that he knew in some dim way he'd been barely outrunning for years. Day after day of idleness led to doubt. Would he be a good father? Did he even want to be a father? Were they having a child to try to save something that was failing? He entertained old regrets. There were other women he might have married. Still, he knew it was more than just his job or his marriage or his lack of any real friendships. It was something bigger. It left him feeling emptied.

He needed work. Sixteen days into the time off, he started taking Wendy's anti-depressants. She couldn't use them because of the baby. "Besides," she said, working her hands over her belly, "I don't think I need them anymore. I feel the best I've ever felt."

Descending the steps, he wondered if maybe the pills were keeping him awake. They certainly weren't making him feel any less dejected.

He inspected the main room of the basement. Drywall, carpeting, recessed lighting, a sectional couch with reclining leg rests, and a huge flat-screen television. Everything was in its place.

He flipped another light switch and started toward the unfinished rooms. In their first house, they'd once had a bat flapping around the basement. Bruce thumped it out of the air with a tennis racket, scooped it up with a fishing net, and then released it outside. The memory kept him on his guard. He waited for something to swoop out of the shadows when he turned on the light to the treadmill room.

Nothing.

He pushed open the door to the sump pump room and groped overhead for the string hanging from the single bulb. Still in the dark, he looked down at something on the floor that lay in the swatch of light coming through the window well. It was a person. Head to the floor. Palms pressed together.

Praying?

Even through the chemical warfare of fear surging through his head and along his spine, Bruce registered a few details. Thin. Ragged clothes. Beard. Long hair.

Turning to flee, he had a vague vision of reaching his cell phone and calling the police. Something happened with his feet. Tangled. He was falling. A brief, blackening pain raged in his forehead.

He wakened slowly up through the layers of unconsciousness. His forehead simmered. Crawling, he found the wall, turned his back to it, and leaned. The cold of the cement seeped through his t-shirt. He held his head with both hands. Black dots floated in the vision of his closed eyes. He moaned.

A voice told him that he should just lie down.

Bruce's eyes flicked open.

A bedraggled man sat on the floor a few feet from him between himself and the door. Bruce's memory came in a rush. Noise in the basement. Sump pump room. An intruder on the floor. He tried to rise, felt the way he was going to pass out, and sank back to the floor. He squeezed the burn in his forehead down to something tolerable. His fear was rabid. He scrambled back into a corner. "Stay the fuck away from me!"

"I'm not going to hurt you."

"Please," Bruce said in a pained whisper. "My wife is pregnant."

"I know," the man said.

Staring out from under his palm, Bruce examined the man. His thinness called to mind branches. His skin pale like an onion. Something on his ankle caught the light. A shackle linked to a chain. Bruce followed the chain to its end. An eye-bolt cemented into the floor. "You're chained?"

The man nodded.

He looked sick. Near death. "Let me out of here," Bruce said.

The man scooted away from the door. "I wasn't trying to stop you."

Bruce tried to rise again, but the dizziness came in blinding waves. He sank back to the floor.

"You might have a concussion."

Bruce sat for a minute until the pain receded and let him think again. "Why are you down here?"

The man looked into Bruce's eyes and then looked at the floor. "I can't really remember," he said. "How does anybody end up anywhere? It just happened. "

Bruce felt dizzy again and swallowed his sudden urge to vomit. "What do you mean, just happened?"

The man rubbed his hand under his nose and, inhaling through it, sounded as though he were congested with a cold. "I don't know any other way to say it."

Testing his pain, Bruce took his hands and nested them in his lap. He closed his eyes and kept the back of his head against the wall. His ears rang with a high-pitched signal, as though being administered a constant hearing test. "This is my house," he said.

"I know that."

Bruce opened his eyes and looked at the chain. The links were thick. Strong. He blinked the man into focus. "I don't understand. How long have you been here? I've owned this house for almost—"

"I was here when the Walkers lived here. Before that, I'm not sure."

Bruce pushed with his elbows and propped himself farther up the wall. He explained that they'd had an inspector come through the house before they closed on it. "How could he have missed ... and, I mean, I've been in this room before, too."

The man smiled callously. "I know."

During spring run-offs and heavy rains, Bruce always checked the sump pump. Ever since carpeting the basement, the threat of water was one of his great fears.

"It's easy to be hidden," the man said, "when nobody really wants to see you to begin with."

Another wave of pain and the black dots returned. Bruce slouched and gripped his forehead. Hearing movement, he opened his eyes. The man was reaching his skeletal arm down into the sump pump well. "What are you—"

He stretched a water-soaked rag toward Bruce. "Hold this against your head."

Bruce studied the dripping rag.

"Just take it."

Eyes shut, he pressed the soaking cold against his forehead, letting the metallic-smelling water run down his face. It cooled the pain. He pulled the rag away and studied it in the dim light.

"There's no blood, but you'll have a bruise."

Too many questions came into his mind. It was impossible to think that a scarecrow of a man lived beneath he and Wendy's coming and goings. "How is this possible ... you being down here?"

The man reached behind him and leaned his arm down into the sump pump well again. When it came up this time, he was holding the cap to a spray paint can. He took a sip from it. "I have water," he said. He held the cap toward Bruce.

"No thanks."

The man finished what was left in the cap. Turning, he moved a small cardboard box in the corner. His right hand hopped a couple times. Turning back, he showed Bruce a cricket pinched between his thumb and fingers. "I get food."

Bruce squinted at the insect. "I sometimes hear them chirping," he said vaguely. "I thought they were outside."

The man opened his mouth, set the cricket in, and bit down on its hard thorax. "There's lots of spiders in the window well, too," he said, swallowing.

Bruce stared. "You can't live like that."

The man set the box back in the corner. "I'm sure I have it better than some people." He picked something else out of the darkness. It was an apple core eaten down to its nucleus of seeds. "Sometimes I have fruit."

Bruce thought for a moment. He looked up and pointed. "Do apples sometimes fall from the tree into the window well?"

"When I'm lucky."

His head felt better, less dizzy. He scooted his back farther up the wall. "Could you open the window?"

The man looked at him. Rising, he turned the bolt lock and pulled. The glass lifted in and up on its creaky hinges.

"That's the sound I heard when I was in bed. You got the apple tonight, didn't you?"

Closing the window again, the man nodded. He crouched.

Bruce's mind flickered, centering on the facts and then rejecting them. "This can't be ... I mean, how did you ... how does something like this happen ... you living down here?"

"I wasn't always here. I remember a mom and a dad and a home." He looked up to the ceiling as though expecting to find a vivid memory there. He shook his head. "It's been too long to remember much about those times."

Another thought came to Bruce. He sniffed, but smelled only basement. "How do you ... I mean, how do you...?"

"Crap and piss?" The man unscrewed the top to a black pipe. "The sewer line's right here."

Bruce nodded. He thought for a moment about what it would be like to live the way this man lived. Who could possibly endure it?

They sat for a moment, each staring at the other. "What do you want?"

The man sat cross-legged on the floor. "Do you have a hack saw?"

He shook his head. "I don't have many tools, but I could buy one."

The man shrugged. "That would be good. I'm not sure where I would go from there, but it's a helluva start."

The central air conditioning unit kicked on and filled the basement with a low hum.

"Are you hungry?"

The man laughed emptily. "What do you think?"

Bruce eased himself up onto his feet. A wave of dizziness came over him. He waited a moment, hands on his knees, and it passed. "I'll be right back," he said.

Working quickly and quietly, he filled a plate. He smeared two pieces of multi-grain bread with peanut butter. He found a tin of sardines and what amounted to a handful of smoked almonds. He grabbed a banana. From the refrigerator, he picked out provolone cheese slices, yogurt, pickles, and a can of diet soda. He went back to the pantry but found only a sleeve of rosemary-flavored water crackers to add to the feast. He started down the stairs, turned back, and poured a full glass of orange juice.

He looked at the plate. Anything else would need cooking. He couldn't risk waking Wendy. Lately, her nose was too keen when it came to the smell of food. How would he explain that there was a man in their basement? He could barely explain it to himself.

He pushed the door open. The room was empty. "Hey?"

Crawling on all fours, he emerged from a dark corner. He sat cross-legged again. "I didn't think you'd come back. Walker never did."

Bruce set the plate and the glass on the floor. "I said I would."

The man laughed. "I can't eat all of this."

"I thought I'd give you some variety." Bruce sat again with his back to the cold wall.

Surveying the meal, he first picked up the orange juice and took gulping drinks. "Jesus Christ," he said, pulling the glass from his lips, "that's good."

Bruce smiled, imagining orange juice after years of eating bugs and drinking mineral-rich water.

The man folded a piece of bread and took a huge bite. His chewing was sticky and slow. He opened the cola and sluiced down the rest. He crunched almonds, snapped off a bite of pickle, and then made himself a few crackers with cheese.

Bruce watched. Neither said anything. The only sounds were the primal moans of satisfaction coming from the man's throat.

He pushed the plate away. "I'll make myself sick," he said. He took the banana, sardines, and yogurt and set them into the darkness behind him. "I'll keep those for later."

Bruce nodded, feeling the tingling of fulfillment that came with knowing what he'd done for this man.

The man leaned back against the opposite wall under the window. He kept his hands on his belly.

"Feels good to help," Bruce said, as much to himself as the other man.

The man sniggered and shook his head. "I almost feel bad for all the hate I've had toward you."

"Hate?"

He nodded, scratching his fingers into his beard. "This isn't the first time you've been here."

Bruce adjusted his back nervously. "I don't understand."

"There's no way you could." The man rubbed his hands, one over the other. He stared ahead, his eyes fixed on nothing. "Sometimes you come down here at night. I never really know when it's going to happen. You beat me."

"Beat you? What are you talking about? I've never hurt another person in my life."

The man explained that Bruce walked in his sleep. He'd come into the sump pump room and hammer down blows with a length of PVC pipe. "Sometimes I pass out it's so bad. Other times it's just a whack or two."

Bruce sat bewildered. "Why would I ... I come in here? I come in here and I hurt you? I don't believe it."

The man sat quietly. The silence rang with the truthfulness of what he'd said.

"Sleepwalking? I have no history of ... I mean, I can't believe that I would..."

The man leaned forward and took another sip of cola. "It's not like you know you're doing it."

Bruce stared at the floor, unable to meet his eyes. "Still, if it's true, it's horrible."

"I wouldn't lie," the man said. "The door has no lock. I do what I can to block it, but it's useless. You're much stronger than me."

They sat in a long silence. The description of his latent violence numbed Bruce. "One of my colleague's daughters used to sleepwalk," he nearly whispered. "The doctor put her on short-acting tranquilizers. I could try that."

The man sat, his eyes glossy with what looked to be remembrance. He blinked and then looked at Bruce. "You should probably go back to bed. It wouldn't do for your wife to wake up and find us down here."

He picked up the plate and stood. "You're right. She wouldn't understand any of this."

"Why, do you?"

"No."

The man smiled and told Bruce to remember his promise.

"My promise?"

He snorted an angry little laugh. "The hack saw?"

"Oh, right. I won't forget."

The man crawled into the darkness and curled himself into a tight ball. "I hope not," he said.

"I won't hurt you anymore, either."

"Just get the saw."

Wendy snored lightly. Bruce lay, trying to sort through what he had seen and heard. His eyes were gritty, and exhaustion weighted his body down, like being buried on a beach. He fought to stay awake. Opening his eyes against the dreamy visions that come before sleep, he told himself that he should stay awake.

He never asked the other man's name. He would tomorrow ... after a stop at the hardware store. He would open the door, holding the saw, and say, "First, I want to know your name."

Rolling on his side, he gathered the sheet up to his chin. His mind went slowly to dreamy musings of Lake Missaukee, then sketchy visions of the meetings in Denver, and then back to the lake.

"Bruce!"

His eyes snapped open into the darkness. The time glowed red in front of him. 5:24.

"Bruce, get up! My water broke!"

Her overnight bag was already packed for a moment like this. Six minutes later, they were in the car. Fifteen minutes more, the hospital. The baby, a boy, came quickly and quietly.

Bruce cut the cord. A nurse set the newborn momentarily on Wendy's chest. Another sucked the mucous from his nose.

He cried out his existence.

"Don't cry, angel," Wendy said, lovingly. "Don't cry."

The doctor removed his gloves. "Good job, Mom. Some women would kill to have a delivery go so smoothly."

Bruce touched his finger along his son's small, pink arm. He lay in an open bed under a radiant warmer, crying out for something to make everything less cold.

A nurse swaddled the tiny boy and picked him up. "You ready to hold him, Dad?"

Bruce cradled his son. His head fit snugly in the crook of his elbow. No simile could describe the fragility of the tiny fingers. He felt the world shrinking down to the eight pounds, seven ounces in his arms. He needed nothing else to make everything make sense. He thanked God for such a blessing.

Later in the morning, Wendy sat propped in a hospital bed eating scrambled eggs. Bruce was rocking their son they'd named Sam. His little face was impossibly beautiful.

Wendy laughed. "What in the world did you do to your head?"

Bruce tried to recall. "I don't know," he said, reaching up to touch his tender forehead. "I couldn't sleep, and I remember getting out of bed to make a snack. I remember pickles and yogurt."

She laughed again. "Sympathy hunger," she said.

"Maybe." He laughed, too. "I guess I hit my head stumbling around the kitchen."

All the stories they'd heard about colic and sleeplessness never came to pass. Sam slept five hours nearly every night and gave them plenty of rest. He lay between them, and when he would wake fussing, Wendy would turn, open her pajama top, and quietly nurse him. He seemed content with this world he'd come in to.

Awake briefly in the darkness, Bruce and Wendy would whisper to each other over the tiny head. They talked about the days they would spend as a family at the cottage. They called up images of Sam playing in the sand, swimming, and eventually water skiing behind the boat. He would have such a good life. Lulled by the sounds of suckling, Bruce would eventually roll over and drift off into a deep sleep.

Renovation

Footsteps groan in the floor and joists above, making the house seem haunted. A voice calls out. Paul leaves his laptop and looks up the stairwell toward the hole. Their cat only used it for a few weeks until they let it outside one night and it never came back.

A face streaked with shadows stares down at him. "We tripped another circuit breaker," it says. The heavy toolbox slides back into its place, blocking out the circle of light. Paul goes to the breaker box. Thunk. The drum sander above starts again, deafening.

He glances at his sons. Small. Skinny. Both are plugged into music. They hold controllers, and armed men on the television respond to the movements of their fingers. Bodies, dropped vicariously by his boys, lay strewn about a battlefield.

How long has it been since he's said anything to either of them? He has barked orders and scolded for bad grades or chores poorly done. He has shouted at them to stop shouting at each other. Has he said anything kind or asked a question?

He inhales and then sighs out a long breath. "I love you guys," he shouts.

The words are smothered by sanding, music, gunfire. The twins stare at the screen, thumbs and fingers like pistons.

He shakes his head and runs his hand through his hair. "You guys should read something!"

They don't respond, and he already knows their counterargument. It's summer, they'd say, and we don't read in the summer. He looks at the basement window and tries to guess the angle of the sun. Could it already be August?

His wife works back by the water heater where she has made a makeshift desk from the Christmas decoration storage bins. Maybe he'll talk to her ... ask her how long they've been down here. Two weeks, now? Three? No, he thinks. Leave her alone. She's working.

He goes back to the glow of his computer and opens dozen of emails.

Bitzy, their Yorkipoo, uses the cat's litter box in the next room. She's trained herself since they've been down in the basement. Paul rips up pages from his old, musty college textbooks to use as litter. He only wishes that the dog would close the loop and bury what she makes.

Paul and his wife face each other on the hide-a-bed couch. Her eyes are closed. Reaching, he finds the buttons of her pajama top and begins to unbutton her. He waits for some kind of exhausted protest. With each button, he realizes that this is what she wants. Spontaneity. No obsequious requests for sex or pitiful hinting. No jokes about Australian banks and needing to make a deposit Down Under. No, she wants this ... him making his desires known through action. Some things are ruined with too much talking.

He moves his hands up and parts her top. His fingertips skim the curves of her breasts. His blood shifts.

"What are you doing?"

Everything about her tone tells him that this is going nowhere. "Isn't it obvious?" he asks.

She points to their sons in sleeping bags on the carpet next to them. Embarrassed, he makes a half-hearted argument.

"I really don't care what the pioneers did or what the Inuit do," Annie says.

He feels her movements in the bed, her hands re-buttoning her top.

"Are you going to do something about that smell?" she asks.

Sighing, he throws the covers off, steps over a son, and shifts his retreating erection. He goes into the laundry room. Blinking in the sudden light, the Yorkipoo looks up at him from her little bed.

"Shut up, Bitzy," he mumbles.

He scoops the dog's turd, drops it in the toilet, and flushes. When he comes back to bed, his wife isn't there. He finds her back by the water heater glowing in laptop light, fingers flicking on the keyboard. He leans against the wall and watches her.

"What site is that?"

She jumps. "God, don't sneak up." She minimizes the window, opens her email window.

"What are you doing? Chatting?"

She turns and glares into his face. "It's a twenty-four hour world. I might as well get some work done now that I can't sleep."

He apologizes and goes back to bed sheepishly. What the hell was he thinking ... trying to have sex in the basement, flanked by their boys, and blanketed in the heady aroma of dog shit. No wonder she seemed disgusted with him.

In another room, the furnace whooshes on. He looks towards the window well covers pasted with the silhouettes of fallen leaves. How had summer already turned into autumn? Why weren't the boys in school? He tries to sleep, but can't. Had they missed the first day? The first week? He leans over the edge of the bed to check the day's date. First, he checks his email. Six messages, two of them from potential clients. He hits reply and types.

Paul stands at the bottom of the stairs. All of their faces in the cat hole look the same to him as they call down their demands. A plumber tells him to turn off the main water supply. "You got no shutoff valves on any of these goddamn sinks."

He apologizes, finds the main supply, and turns it tight. Ear glowing with a Bluetooth, Annie stands over the boys sitting at a card table. An erratic beat bleeds out from their headphones. Their sullen eyes are bent to the pages of books.

"You got them to read?" he asks, coming into the room.

Not looking at him, Annie nods.

He crosses his arms. "Every one of these guys we've hired has an attitude. You'd think we weren't paying them out the nose."

She still doesn't look. "Jerry says that whoever built this place had no idea what they were doing."

"Who's Jerry?"

She looks at him with palpable disappointment. "The contractor, Paul."

He shrugs. "I don't care about their names. I just want them to finish."

Both boys pull an earbud out and look at Annie.

"That guy just flicked him in the nuts," Eric says. "He's a pimp, isn't he?"

Annie inhales, nods.

The twins look at each other and laugh. "Maurice is badass," Bobby says, smiling.

She points. "Just keep reading and watch the language."

The boys reinsert their music.

He steps closer. "They're reading the same book?"

She nods. *Catcher in the Rye.* You'd think there hasn't been one other good book written since 1951." She shakes her head. "I remember reading it in high school."

"They're reading it for school?" Have the boys been leaving the basement? He looks at sunshine coming dully through a window well cover dusted with snow. "Why aren't they in school, now? Is it Saturday? I can't keep track of—"

"In school? To have them around their 'friends' again? Relive that twelve weeks of hell? I know this isn't ... but, we agreed." She looks at him. "Has it really been any burden for you, anyway?"

What's she talking about? "We've been down here twelve weeks already?"

Her Bluetooth rings. She answers and then covers the earpiece. "I have to take this," she whispers. "Watch them. I'm giving the exam on Friday." She retreats, talking. "I already have most of it done," she says to whomever is on the line with her. Out of the room, she laughs. It's a sound he hasn't heard in a long time.

Watching his boys read, he thinks of them as good boys and is proud of the job they've done with them. They're growing up, he thinks.

Footsteps pound above. The plumber's profanity is audible in the cold air return.

Shaking his head, Paul takes his laptop into the basement bathroom, pulls down his pants, sits, and checks email. Three more new clients want quotes. He low balls the work, thinking of the cost of the plumbing. Trying to type, trying to push through his constipation, he yells for the boys to shut up. A moment later, he hears the opening notes of their video game console booting on the television. They turn the sound down quickly, and he smiles at their courtesy. The subsequent gunfire is muted. They're good boys, he thinks.

Asbestos. The old tiles under the kitchen's linoleum floor are made of asbestos. And, in rough shape ... most likely friable. The contractor says that they can seal the basement door for the removal. The family will be perfectly safe. "It won't be cheap," he says. "Gotta bring in a whole different crew for an operation like that. It's going to add some time, too."

Paul locks himself in the tiny room that houses their water softener. He spends hours, days, weeks turning up new customers, offering ridiculously low prices, promising nearly impossible turn-around times. His client list swells. He ignores the knocking and pleading. When he knows his family is asleep, he orders food online. Most of the delivery places already know to bring deliveries to a basement window. He leans against a wall, chews pizza or Chinese food, and watches his family sleep. The boys always look big in their sleeping bags. All the work, he thinks, it's for them.

Paul wakes up, shifts, tries to find a way to fall back to sleep. The pressure from his bladder is a simmering insistence, and no position helps. He throws off the covers, steps over Eric, and heads to the bathroom. At the top of the stairs, Annie crouches at the cat hole. She's in her bathrobe talking with one of the workers.

"Jerry ... I don't ... I don't understand. We—"

"It's not good ... for either of us."

He slides the toolbox across the opening. Annie crumples, weeps.

"Annie?"

She jumps and then looks down the stairs. "Oh, Paul..." She comes down to him. Her bathrobe is open, revealing her bra and panties.

He closes her robe, looks for the tie, but it's gone. "Don't be like this in front of them, Annie. That's what guys like that dream about ... lonely, vulnerable wives of other men."

She falls against him, sobbing. "I'm sorry, Paul. I'm so sorry."

He holds her, not knowing how long it's been since they've been so close. "It's okay," he says, chuckling at the intensity of her crying. "They'll be done soon." He looks at the dark window wells. "I mean, it's the middle of the night and he's here working. That's good, right?"

She holds him tighter. "It's all too much."

He slips his arms inside her robe, feels the flesh of her back under his fingers. After a moment, he lets his hands slide down into her panties, cups her ass, squeezes.

She looks up, kisses him fiercely. "You're right," she says, "you're right."

He kisses back hungrily, as he did during the first times. They step over Eric and fall into the bed.

She pulls him on top of her.

He pushes himself up, stands. "I'll be right back."

"Paul."

"Really, I'll be right back. Just a quick bit of business to take care of."

"Just stay with me. Please."

Without answering, he rushes to the bathroom. The release is almost as good as the release he imagines will come when he returns to bed. He flushes, guessing that the noises he has made will explain why he had to leave. He rushes back to her.

She's gone.

"Annie?" he whispers. "Annie?"

"Dad, will you shut up," Eric says, "I'm trying to sleep."

Paul doesn't have the strength to reprimand his son's rudeness. He lets his head fall back against the pillow. How did things get so complicated, so broken? His own tears come.

In the day, everything is footsteps. Upstairs the workers come and go ... dragging, rolling, and lugging equipment. If not on her laptop, Annie is in the workout room on the treadmill. Her feet boom against the belt, her face a sheen of sweat. Paul stands in the doorway and watches her. She pushes her hair with her hands, whips it away with snaps of her neck.

"I could cut it for you," he shouts.

She doesn't answer, doesn't even look at him. Her ears are plugged up with headphones.

He walks away.

Heat radiates through the bottom of a pizza box into Paul's palm. He ducks into the water softener room and checks his email one more time. Coming out, he sees the twins at the window of the workshop. Eric passes up a wad of money, and a hand comes through the window and takes it.

"Boys," he says, "I already paid for the pizza."

Eric looks at him, disgusted. Bobby's face is kinder. "Okay, Dad," he says.

"Come on, I thought we'd find something good on television." His boys look tall and he's happy that, despite the lack of fresh air, they've had quite a growth spurt down here.

"Sure, Dad," Bobby says.

A moment later, they come into the room where Paul sits on the couch. Eric grabs the pizza box, taking all of the pieces except the one that Paul holds in his hand. He walks off to the laundry room.

"If it's okay, Dad, we'll eat in here," Bobby says.

"You don't have to ask his goddamn permission," Eric calls out.

Paul says it's okay. Annie is back by the water heater typing away on her keyboard. Anymore, she only eats the prepackaged dietary meals that she's been having delivered. The deep freezer is filled with them.

It feels so long since they've eaten a meal together.

He walks around the empty spaces of the basement, gathering pizza boxes, Chinese food containers, chip bags, and pop bottles. Opening a window behind the furnace, he launches the garbage out onto the lawn. He pushes hard against the refuse that's already there and wonders why the contractor's men can't clean up the yard.

He begins to watch a movie, gets anxious with his idleness, and goes back to his computer. When he emerges from his improvised office, the basement windows are black, and he isn't sure if it's the same blackness from when he went in or if it's been light and then gone back to dark again.

The boys huddle in the laundry room. They have the exhaust hose disconnected from the dryer. Bobby has it up to his face and is laughing into it.

Paul smiles, imagining the noise they must be making outside. "Having fun, boys?"

They both jump. Bobby takes the hose from his face and a dusting of dryer lint remains circled around his mouth.

His sheepish look triggers something in Paul. "You really shouldn't mess around with appliances like that. It's dangerous."

Eric looks at Bobby. "Look who's suddenly playing at being a dad."

Paul steps farther into the room. "Eric, your mouth lately—"

Eric steps forward into Paul's face. They are eye to eye. "What about my mouth, Dad?" He shakes his head, smirks. "Just get the hell out of here."

Paul grabs what turns out to be Eric's meaty upper arm. "Now look—"

With suddenness and a surprising strength, Eric grabs Paul's wrist, turns him, and twists his arm behind his back. He walks him forward and presses his cheek against the laundry room wall.

"Come on, Eric," Bobby says, "let him go."

"Do what you do best, Dad," Eric hisses in Paul's ear, "and leave us alone." He moves him to the doorway, pushes him out, and slams the door.

Paul rubs his elbow. It's this basement, he thinks. This goddamn basement. We've been down here too long. It's making us crazy.

He sprints up the stairs, pounds on the door. "Let us up, now! When the hell are you going to be finished?" His words are lost under the whining of saw blades spinning through wood, hammers banging, men shouting to each other.

Someone finally comes to the door in answer to his pounding. He hears explanations: Asbestos in the attic insulation. Paint fumes in the living room. Black mold behind most of the old drywall. Nearly all of the first floor has been stripped down to the studs.

A new cost estimate slips under the door.

Paul weeps. At the bottom of the stairs, looking up at him in a white sports bra and white running shorts, Annie resembles a ghost with her pale skin.

They look at each other.

"I do love you," he says.

Are those tears or sweat running down her cheeks? She adjusts the earbud in her left ear and walks away.

Thin and ragged, Bitzy comes and looks up the stairs at him.

Someone needs to feed that dog, he thinks. First, he examines the new cost estimate. Most of the prices have doubled, some tripled. He runs down the stairs to the water softener room, ignoring the laughing of his boys, the wretchedness of the dog, the silence of his wife. We just need them to finish, he thinks. We'll be fine once we get upstairs. In between the work he does for existing clients, he scavenges the Internet looking for more. He outbids anyone, piling himself with accounts for which he will be paid peanuts. He orders food and takes the deliveries directly from the workshop and into his tiny workspace. Curled around the water softener, he sleeps in a sleeping bag five hours at a time before waking again to sixteen-hour work days.

Paul walks by the stairwell one morning, looks, and discovers the basement door open.

"Hello?" he calls, standing halfway up the stairs. "Anybody here?"

He goes up to the kitchen, looking for tools, equipment ... any sign that the men might still be working.

Nothing.

He runs back downstairs to tell his family that they can finally leave. Searching every room, he finds nobody. The boys probably bolted the minute they saw the door open, and he doesn't blame them. Probably out on their bikes tearing up the neighborhood.

He's hurt that Annie went up without him. They've had their troubles, but he imagined a tour of their newly renovated home might make a nice metaphor ... a mutual look at the way a thing can be wrecked and ugly and then put back together better than before.

Upstairs, everything is as they once dreamed it would be. In the kitchen, stainless steel appliances, granite countertops, an island with a butcher block top. Both bathrooms have pedestal sinks, Jacuzzi baths, and huge glassed-in showers. Their bedroom has a new walk-in closet, cedar storage, and shelves for dozens of pairs of shoes.

"Annie," he calls into the space. She's not there.

The boxy rooms of the old layout have been replaced with an open floor plan. The kitchen looks out onto a dining area which opens up into a great room with shining hardwood floors.

He walks up to the huge picture window. He touches his fingers along the frame and says the name of the high-end window brand ... a name he and Annie used to say to each other when they would feel the winter breeze seeping through their old aluminum windows. In the past, they spoke the window company's name reverently, as though it were a deity.

And now, his entire house was filled with such windows. He swells with pride for what they have accomplished.

The front door opens behind him.

Annie.

She's holding a suitcase. He imagines her taking loads of clothes up from the basement in it ... hers, his, the boys'.

He smiles. "I'll help in just a minute."

"Bitzy ran away," she says.

"The house is beautiful, isn't it?" he says. His wife isn't so easily distracted or comforted. "Don't worry," he says. "She'll be back."

"No she won't," she says, turning and walking out the door.

Paul turns back to the window and looks at the garbage covering the backyard. He imagines the yellowing or already dead grass beneath it. Thinking of the bald patches of lawn, he touches his fingers over his scalp and finds mainly skin, a narrow horseshoe of hair around the sides and back of his head.

Something comes to him, an image from another house ... not the one before this one or the one before that ... the first one, the one they'd rented. He remembers the horrible carpeting and how they'd begged the landlord to let them pull it up. Beneath it they found hardwood floor, dry and cracking. Annie had spent four nights in a row rubbing oil into it, bringing it back to some kind of life. He remembers sitting on that floor, their infant twins not far from him on a blanket, and his wife behind him, legs spread eagle around him. She would give him haircuts, being frugal so they could save for a house of their own.

It's a precious memory, and he tries to remember the feeling of her fingers in his hair. Smiling, he looks behind him at the door ... hoping she'll be home soon from walking the dog.

Load

Crowe listened to the superintendent and the super's wife in the cold-air return. He wanted news of deliveries or renovations. He wanted specific apartment numbers.

Instead their talk was the same endless stream that it had been for years:

I can't trust you.

You lie.

Youspyonme.

Youkeepsecrets.

Youkeepmoneyfromme.

Youreadmydiary

You'refatandlazy

Youturnthetenantsagainstme

Crowe went into the bathroom and came out with a towel. He stuffed it into the vent and the voices disappeared. He imagined the super and his wife, each sequestered in different rooms of their basement apartment, an ocean of hate between them.

Falling into bed again, he felt the exhaustion from another fruitless day on the upper floors, knocking on doors, imploring tenants to consider the weight of their things. There were rumors of new hot tubs, new gas fireplaces with stone mantles, new deep freezers. Nobody cared. Some slammed their doors. Others opened their doors only as wide as their chain locks would allow. They admitted to having heard the rumors and load warnings too, but what could be done? Others confronted him. They'd earned their money and it was their right to spend it however they wanted. They didn't want to hear about the size of the cracks in the ground-level apartments. Air pockets, they countered, when he explained that one part of the building had sunk two inches in six years. Buildings settle into soft soil. It's perfectly natural. It was as though they had memorized the Board's letters of assurance.

Predictions of a complete collapse made most laugh or shake their heads. Doom and gloom, they said, pointing out their windows towards the building's buttressing exoskeleton. They spoke confidently of the Board's twenty new steel pilings, despite reports that less than five pilings had been properly installed.

Crowe countered with the arguments that he and Dagmar had concocted. She was more militant than he was, but he was more persuasive in person. The foundation had never been constructed for so many residents, their excessive belongings, or the addition of more floors. Some listened, and he gave these tenants his name and his phone number in addition to his pamphlets.

The telephone rattled Crowe from his half-sleep.

"I need help," an old man's voice said.

Crowe blinked at the itchy fatigue in his eyes. "What?"

"I fell. I can't get back into bed."

Crowe sighed. "Sir, I'm so tired. Can't you—"

"I called other numbers. They hung up."

Crowe sat up against the dead weight of his body. "What apartment are you in?"

The old man gave him a number. Seventeen flights up.

Crowe imagined the climb. "There's nobody else?"

"Just my aide. She doesn't come until the afternoon."

Crowe threw his legs over the side of his bed and shuffled his feet in the darkness until he stirred up his pants. "Okay."

"I'll push the key under the door," said the old man.

Crowe imagined a skinny, grizzled body inching pathetically across the floor to the apartment's threshold. "Hold tight. I'm on my way."

In the stairwell, he took the steps two at a time.

In the morning, he woke to shouting coming up through the cold air return and leaking through the muffling towel:

I hate you.

Ihateyou.

Youarealiar

Eatmyshit

Gotohell

Crowe rose from the bed, knowing he wouldn't fall asleep again. It was Sunday. People were always home on Sunday. He had work to do.

He lifted the towel.

Ihateyou!Ihateyou!IhateyouIwishyouweredead...

Waiting for coffee to brew, he remembered the old man from the night before. Crowe had opened the door and found all shivering ninety-five pounds of him lying on the floor with the entry rug draped over his bony torso.

"I am so thirsty," the old man said.

Crowe picked him up and delivered him back to his bed. A moment later, he brought him a glass of water. "Is this what you wanted?"

"You're a good man," he said, patting the back of Crowe's hand with his cold fingers.

Crowe stayed until the old man was breathing the regular, raspy breaths of sleep. He let himself out, locked the door behind him, and slid the key back under the door.

Now, sipping coffee, Crowe fingered the growing, jagged crack that ran from his own floor nearly all the way to his ceiling. He showered, grabbed his pamphlets, and headed for the stairwell, hoping to get to the topmost floors today. Ascending, he thought of the old man's thankful eyes. He wondered what his own parents would have been like in their old age. They had died when he was still young, when a major shift in the building snapped a gas line and asphyxiated them in their sleep. He had taken their apartment and their problems.

Crowe climbed until he came to a point where the emergency stairwell was blocked by a locked gate. He opened the fire door and stepped onto the sixty-first floor. An overweight security guard met him. Feeling tight heat along the base of his neck, Crowe handed the man an envelope. The guard took it. He glanced behind him into the empty hallway that narrowed towards a tiny vanishing point. The guard then turned back to Crowe, taking a cursory glance at his shoes, his dress pants, his satchel, his tie, and finally his neatly combed hair.

"What you selling?"

Crowe glanced at the envelope in the guard's hand. "Right now, my hope is to buy."

Nodding, the guard opened the envelope, ran the tip of a sausage finger along the edges of cash, and then stuffed it in his pants pocket. "Anyone asks, you tell them you managed to sneak in while I was on another floor."

"Of course."

The guard unlocked the gate, relocked it behind him, and then vanished.

A moment later as Crowe passed the service elevator, there was a bing, the doors slid open, and two men wrestled out a goliath, rubberized mattress. Crowe followed them at a distance as they struggled and swore their way down the hall. They soon stopped and rapped on a door.

A young man dressed in a business suit opened it.

"This is the last of it," the biggest of the delivery men said.

Nodding, the young man stepped aside to let them in. He stood in the doorway watching their progress, telling them to be careful of the statue in the living room.

"Excuse me, sir," Crowe said.

The man gave him a quick onceover. "Yes?"

"That's a big bed." He cleared his throat. "Do you live alone?"

Frowning, the man looked down the hallway. "Where is that fat assed security guard?" He looked at Crowe. "What do you care about my big bed? You turning tricks or something?"

Crowe reached into his satchel, flipped through papers, and then produced a pamphlet. He handed it to the man. The title read, *What You Need to Know about Waterbeds and Load.*

The man looked at it. "Oh Christ ... get out of my face."

"Sir, that bed will add nearly a ton of load once it's filled. I just want you to consider the—"

The delivery men came out again. The man turned away from Crowe.

The burly men assessed the situation. "This guy bothering you?" one of them asked.

The young man shook his head and then traded the pamphlet for the delivery receipt clipboard. He signed.

The delivery man studied the warnings. Looking Crowe coldly in the eye, he shredded the pamphlet into pieces. He took the clipboard back and smiled menacingly at Crowe.

"Enjoy that bed, sir."

The man nodded. Walking away, one of the delivery men whispered in the other's ear. Looking back at Crowe, he shook his head.

Crowe's pulse beat in his ears.

The other man went back into his apartment and closed the door. After a moment, Crowe sighed, took another pamphlet from his satchel, and slipped it under the man's door.

He spent the next hour knocking on other doors, trying to get people to sign petitions, trying to get them to take pamphlets, trying to get them to listen. Door after door slammed in his face.

Then he hit the jackpot. A door opened to reveal Mr. Russell Scott standing before him, a younger member of the building's Board and the firebrand who had spearheaded the push for the steel pilings that reinforced the building's exoskeleton.

Crowe cleared his throat. "Mr. Scott?"

Mr. Scott studied him for a moment. "Yes? Can I help you?"

Crowe extended his hand and introduced himself. He had one shot. "I am with a group of concerned tenants who—"

Mr. Scott's face turned serious and dismissive. "Board business is for Board meetings. I can't speak to you right now."

"Sir, if you could—"

"Contact the Board secretary to get on the agenda."

"What I have to say would only take a minute. Please—"

Mr. Scott started to close his door.

Crowe reached out, only to get his fingers caught between the closing door and the doorjamb. Yelping, he pulled his hand free and fell back against the wall. He grasped his wounded fingers and squeezed at the pulsing pain. Eyes closed, he slumped down to the floor.

"Are you okay?"

Crowe imagined what Dagmar would do in his place. She'd sweep Scott's legs and bring him down like a condemned building. Grabbing him by the lapels, she'd hold her reddened fingers in his face. "This?" she'd say. "This is nothing. I'd bite them off if it meant that you'd listen, you sonuvabitch!"

Dagmar worried Crowe. Following her lead, some tenants had started going to the building's receiving docks and slashing the tires of delivery trucks. How could that lead to anything good?

Crowe let go of his fingers and turned them in the air in front of him. Blood seeped from two of the bludgeoned knuckles. "The Board secretary never puts us on the agenda. We've asked," he said, wincing as he tried to flex his hand.

Mr. Scott crouched down and took Crowe's hand in his. He turned it back and forth, examining it. "How bad?"

"I don't think it's broken."

Mr. Scott released Crowe's hand. "So what is so damn important?" he asked, smiling.

Crowe reached for his satchel. He had a board member listening to him. He had to go big.

Panic rooms. An apartment invasion occurred a year ago on the thirty-eighth floor. The tenant was beaten into a coma and woke three weeks later severely brain-damaged. "Since the incident," Crowe said, "more and more people on the upper floors are having panic rooms built."

"I know," Mr. Scott said. "The Board gave the okay. The weight issues are negligible."

"Negligible," Crowe said, "if people follow the code, which allows for replacing one wooden door and doorjamb with steel on one existing interior room. That's not what's happening."

Crowe reached into his satchel and showed Mr. Scott a copy of blueprints that Dagmar had obtained. It called for the demolition of walls to an existing room to be replaced with three-inch-thick steel walls reinforced by concrete. He tapped the piece of paper. "Mr. Scott, we're talking about twenty tons of additional weight per room ... at least."

Mr. Scott crossed his arms. "I find it a little hard to believe—"

"We have evidence that at least three such rooms exist." Crowe raised his index finger. "And, we have a witness ... an electrician who wired just such a room up on the seventieth floor."

Looking grave, Mr. Scott stood up slowly. "And so what would you have the Board do?"

Crowe rose, too, stuffing the blueprints back into his satchel. "Enforce the code," he said. "Have any existing panic rooms demolished at the owners' expense. Establish only one receiving area with a checkpoint to examine all incoming items, especially building materials." Crowe crossed his arms. "If something isn't done, this whole place will undoubtedly collapse on itself, exoskeleton or not."

Mr. Scott scratched his chin. "You'd be willing to brief the Board about this?"

Crowe smiled. "We've been trying to speak to the Board for over five years."

He wrote down Crowe's contact information and promised that he would be in touch personally. "If it can be arranged, I'll want you to bring those blueprints ... and that electrician."

Smiling, Crowe nodded.

That evening, he sat at his small table eating a bowl of shrimp-flavored fried noodles. He nodded, snapped open his eyes, and soon nodded off again.

The telephone rang.

"Mr. Crowe, this is Russell Scott of the Board. I've talked to each member, and a narrow majority has voted you onto the agenda for Thursday."

"I'll be there."

"Some of your listeners will be quite resistant. They'll need to hear everything."

"I'll bring the works."

Hanging up, Crowe immediately punched in another number. Dagmar answered, and he told her the good news.

"I'll come over tonight and help you with your presentation," she said. "We'll make them quake."

Crowe beamed. Feeling fully awake, he opened his satchel and found everything related to panic rooms, spreading out the materials on his table.

Ihateyou.Ican'tlivelikthis. Idon'ttrustyou. Liar. You're keepingsecrets. You'resleepingaround.You'respyingonme. You'retheworstthingthateverhappenedtome.Iwishyouwere dead...

Crowe dropped two towels over the voices of the super and his wife. He wrote his speech and then rehearsed it.

"Panic rooms are a knee-jerk reaction to an isolated incident. Of course, ladies and gentlemen of the Board, that doesn't mean we shouldn't be panicked." Crowe paced. "What should panic us are the panic rooms themselves. With your permission let me describe—"

There was a knock at his door. Expecting Dagmar, he instead saw three bearded men standing at his threshold.

"Yes?"

A fist landed in his stomach like a brick. Crowe lay on the ground, struggling to breathe against the spasm of his diaphragm. The men came into his apartment, closed the door behind them, and circled around him.

"Wish you had a panic room now, don't you?"

One of the men went to Crowe's table, gathered his papers and the blueprints into his satchel, and slung it over his shoulder.

Another of the men crouched down close. "You're not going to go to that Board meeting. Right?"

A boot landed in Crowe's kidneys. His vision blackened.

When he opened his eyes, he was in his bed. His lower back throbbed. Dagmar sat in a chair near him. "The bastards didn't get anything we can't replace," she said.

Crowe tried to sit up. Pain put him down again. "Do we have a spare set of kidneys?" He winced. Talking hurt.

Dagmar laughed, pushing her hand through her silver bangs. "Believe it or not, this is good. It means they're scared."

Crowe rubbed his sore guts. "Who were they?"

She shrugged. "Thugs. Hired by the panic room contractors or hired by some Board member getting kickbacks from the contractors."

Crowe stared at her black military boots.

"I'll have someone camp outside your door tonight. You can sleep easy." She stood. "Excellent job today, Crowe."

After she left, Crowe thought over what she'd said. She was right. People were scared. The Board was going to listen. They were going to put an end to panic rooms. Maybe they would even listen to their other concerns. An end to excessive furniture, weight lifting equipment, grand pianos...

Ican'tstandyouanymore!Ican'tlivelikethisIhate everythingaboutyou...

Crowe looked at the vent. The idea of trying to cover it made his body ache. Please shut up, he thought. Please just let me sleep. He wondered if maybe, in addition to the moratorium on panic rooms, he could talk the Board into firing the superintendent. He'd heard, though, that the super's contract was airtight. He was personal friends with some of the Board members.

Suddenly, their stream of suspicion and hate became coherent conversation.

"What is that? What is that!?"

"Dynamite, Anya. I can end your misery right now."

"Asshole, you'd kill us both."

"So much the better ... like Romeo and Juliet. Though Romeo and Judas is more like it."

Silence.

"Fine, Sam. Let's do it right then. Give me a stick ... we'll end it together. Oh happy dagger!"

Crowe strained his ears in the quiet that followed, waiting for them to keep bickering and, for the first time, hoping for it. The walls pinged and ticked with the building's settling. Crazy assholes, he thought. If they didn't waste so much time fighting with each other, the super might actually be able to repair some of these cracks.

Shaking his head, he tried to fall asleep.

An hour later, wretched with insomnia, he propped himself up against the headboard. Air whirred and hummed in the vents. He waited, listened, wanting something. Anything. Would he even hear it? Would anyone? The tiny flick of a lighter's wheel. Spark meeting butane. The hiss of a fuse.

He recalled what he could of the speech he had prepared.

"Ladies and Gentlemen of the Board, let us consider the mayhem of a building this size crushing itself from the top down..."

For effect, his speech opened with graphic detail about the coming devastation. He couldn't bring himself to repeat it out loud.

The Neighborhood® Division

Stone Montgomery, president of OptimiCorp's Neighborhood division, used to drive to the meetings and sit down with the residents face-to-face. At least that's what Joe Hainer had heard. They say that Montgomery helped the original Neighborhood families unload their U-Hauls and moving vans. That was decades ago. Joe and his son lived in California's seventh Neighborhood project. Anymore, Montgomery met with the various resident groups through video conferencing.

Joe checked his cell phone. In two minutes Stone Montgomery's impressive face would be on the big screen. Squared-jaw. Broad smile. Good head of hair with just enough gray to hint at his wisdom. Joe wanted to meet Montgomery in person. He wanted to see him the same way he wanted to see the Grand Canyon or the JadeCorp Building in Chicago. Montgomery seemed like something big.

The others sipped coffee quietly. The sounds of the Neighborhood community center filled the room. The arrhythmic ricochet and return of a racquetball game. The occasional crash of someone dropping their dumbbells or barbells. Joe glanced at Zach Watson, whose eye twitched every time a weight hit the padded floor—an infraction of the weight room rules. Watson had initiated getting the rules posted on every wall.

Joe liked best the tinny, high-pitched sounds echoing above the pool. He tried to hear his son's voice in the chaos of happiness. His thoughts drifted to Stevie more and more lately. Stevie always swam while Joe attended the monthly meetings. In any other neighborhood, Joe guessed that his fourteen-year-old would want nothing to do with his father. He'd pass on swimming and instead choose virtual games, or the Ultranet, or maybe even vandalism or drugs. Stevie's growing up in the Neighborhood had nurtured him into a fine young man, Joe was sure of it. The boy was pleasant to be around. None of Joe's colleagues ever described their teenagers as pleasant. Demonic maybe, but not pleasant.

"Good evening, everybody," Stone Montgomery said. "How are you, Joe?"

Each person offered greetings to Montgomery's large, congenial face on the wall-length video screen. Joe smiled. Montgomery had remembered his name.

When Montgomery opened the floor, Zach Watson's hand went up like clockwork. The others rolled their eyes or looked away. Bill Anderson, the local Whip, confirmed that Zach had indeed signed up to speak.

"Mine is more of a question than a concern," Zach started. He smoothed his hand over a stack of papers in front of him. "I guess I was just wondering how much time someone is allowed to spend in his backyard."

Something sparked along Joe's spine.

Montgomery studied Zach. He exhaled. "This seems like a question that could be answered by reading the community bylaws."

"I did," Zach said, his voice already obsequious and defensive. "There wasn't anything specific regarding the amount—"

"What are you getting at, Watson?"

Stone Montgomery smiled down upon them. "Let's not forget our courtesy, Bill." He then turned to Zach. "Maybe it would help for you to get more specific with your conce—your question. We have other business yet tonight."

Joe watched Zach's nervous fingers—scratching his ears, his nose, his neck. What was he up to?

"This isn't just my question." Zach always seemed to be representing some invisible group. "Others asked me to bring this up tonight, too." He scooted his chair closer to the table. "We have just noticed that Mike Fredericks spends a great deal of time in his backyard. It just seems—"

"Oh, this is bullsh—" Bill caught himself. "Really, Watson. The guy has a two-year old. It's not like he's building a deck back there. I mean, can he keep his son away from the road and let him play in the backyard? Is that okay with you?"

Zach turned toward Stone Montgomery. "We're just thinking in terms of the front yard quota."

Montgomery smiled and cleared his throat. "Of course, Mr. Watson, we all appreciate your concern. Diligence and watchfulness are sometimes necessary to make the Neighborhood work. But, in this case, I must concur with Bill. Mr. Frederick's actions seem quite innocuous—even expected for a young father."

Zach slumped into a retreat. His hands flopped around in front of him like baby birds trying to launch themselves from the table. "That's why we offered it as a question. A few of us were just wondering." He landed his hands into his lap.

Joe's adrenaline settled. He exhaled. Nothing had come of Watson's trivial complaint. Sometimes Joe's colleagues at work on the outside asked him how things were in Stepford. Other times they called it Jonestown. It was unfair. The Neighborhood was a blessed place—a revolutionary philosophy in living.

Still, he was bothered that Bill was the one that had jumped so quickly to Mike's defense. Only the week before Mike had sprung from his front porch at the sight of Joe pulling a rented moving truck into the driveway. He helped Joe remove an old refrigerator and then wrestle in the new one. It took over an hour.

Mike was a good neighbor. Why hadn't Joe defended him?

Montgomery surveyed the room silently for a moment. "If that represents the concerns for this month, I would like to get right to new business."

Joe recognized something in Montgomery's face. Nervousness. It was something that Joe saw more often in his own face lately. Closing the back door of his house gingerly, he would skulk into the bathroom after a late-night cigarette in the backyard. He looked at himself in the mirror as he pistoned the toothbrush through his mouth. He saw an anxious man.

"I'm sure you've all heard," Stone Montgomery started, "and I can assure you that what you've been hearing has been exaggerated by the media."

Joe wasn't the only one in the dark. The faces in the room suggested that nobody knew what Montgomery was talking about.

Montgomery seemed bolstered by their ignorance. "Let me just say that the allegations against OptimiCorp are without veracity or tangible evidence." He explained that a watchdog group was accusing the company of environmental abuses in its SafeWaughter operations on the Great Lakes.

"OptimiCorp will very likely need to go to court over the allegations, but the proceedings will in no way affect the way of life we have come to value."

Montgomery turned his gaze deliberately from one person to the next as he continued speaking. "What we have here in the Neighborhood experiment is momentous, revolutionary and, to be frank, exclusive. Ideas that are momentous, revolutionary, and exclusive have a history of being reviled. We will be attacked." He cleared his throat. "By government agencies, by the media, and sometimes by the courts. There are those who will look for our weaknesses in order to destroy us. We must, however, be strong. What the Neighborhood represents is worth fighting for. I, for one, cherish what we have. I can't say that about many of the products available in the market today."

Montgomery's words were soundtracked by the jubilant shouting from the pool, the report of the racquetball game, the canon crashes from the weight room. Joe was washed over with the feeling of his good fortune.

"And," Montgomery continued, "I would like to announce that we will likely soon have our first Neighborhood university. Neighborhood professors. Neighborhood staff. We could break ground on a site in the San Francisco project within a few months."

People around the table applauded.

Joe pictured his son's shiny, youthful body walking around the pool deck and over to the diving board. He would jump with confidence, sink in a column of bubbles, and then rise again into arms and legs that would make the surface work for him.

"There's only one more piece of new business," Bill Anderson announced. "Joe Hainer has indicated that he would like to speak."

Joe swallowed. He had signed up to speak right before the meeting started. He shifted in his seat. "If we could," he began, "I would like to table the proposal for next time."

Bill wrote something down. "So noted." He smiled at the group. "Next month's meeting..."

"Just a moment, Bill," Montgomery said. He looked at Joe. "Could we at least know the nature of what we are tabling?"

Joe looked into Montgomery's furrowed brow and stern eyes. His face grew warm. "It was really more of a quest—" He glanced at Zach Watson. "It's just some thoughts I have about the Fire Sentinel proviso."

Montgomery considered him long enough that a drop of sweat broke from under Joe's arm and slid down his ribs. "Well, I guess we'll have to see what that's about next month," he said.

Joe stayed in his seat long after Bill adjourned the meeting. He looked at the dark screen where Montgomery had been only ten minutes before, glowering at him as though he were something foul he had stepped in.

The Fire Sentinel proviso.

To keep influences out, the Neighborhood provided almost everything. Schools. A hospital. Garbage pickup. Soon, a university. Almost every Neighborhood had a plumber or a carpenter or a mason living in it, and these were the people residents hired when they needed someone. At times, if necessary, OptimiCorp transported someone from another Neighborhood. The only service they couldn't provide was firefighting. The Neighborhood experienced few fires. It was counterintuitive, the bylaws explained, to pay competitive wages for firefighting in such an environment. Hence, the proviso.

In less than two years, at sixteen, Stevie would be trained to be a Neighborhood Fire Sentinel. Every child, boy or girl, fell under the proviso. They received training and then minimum wage for two years, which many used toward college.

Sometimes the thorough training helped a few of them land firefighting jobs on the outside.

Joe had never given the proviso much thought. Fires were so infrequent that they often had the sentinels walk the inside perimeter of the wall to pick up trash that outsiders sometimes tossed over. Glorified trash stabbers, or so Joe had always thought.

Two months ago, a journalist from a muckraking newspaper did a story about a boy in the San Diego Neighborhood. He had died while fighting a fire. Crushed under a fallen ceiling and then burned to death. He was seventeen. A colleague from work had shown Joe the article.

"Hey, Dad, up and at 'em," Stevie called from the doorway of the conference room.

The young man leaned into the room. No shirt. Flushed face. Damp, shaggy hair. He was impossibly sublime—like something just born.

"Right behind you, kiddo."

Joe found a note under his windshield wiper:

There are many who have had questions about that proviso. We're behind you.

It was unsigned.

Joe crouched into a corner of his backyard later that night where he was quite certain he couldn't be seen from any of the windows of his neighbors' houses. He lit a cigarette, hoping to let go of some of the tension that seemed to spasm in his back and shoulders. The weeping willow shimmied in a slight spring breeze. Joe shivered.

He and Hanna had a weeping willow in their first backyard on the outside. He remembered looking out his window one windy day and watching his neighbor. Every time the willow branches leaned over the fence in the gusts of wind, the neighbor hacked them off with a pair of shears. "I can trim any branches that hang over my side," he said, when Joe had confronted him.

Another time, seeing a new neighbor working on his truck in the driveway, Joe crossed the street to introduce himself. The man came out from under the hood holding a wrench like a war mattock. He stared into Joe's face. "What the hell do you want?"

According to their realtor, it was a good neighborhood. It probably was for her. There were always at least three "for sale" signs somewhere on the street. Nobody really knew anybody. Strangers came and went and were replaced by more strangers.

A few years and a few promotions later, Joe was able to move his family into an exclusive neighborhood in an affluent part of town. Other than the houses and the lawns, the new neighborhood wasn't much better than the first. People barricaded themselves in 5,000 square foot homes, only to refinish and carpet the basement to descend into deeper seclusion and larger televisions. The newsletter was full of petty complaints about someone noticing that someone else hadn't hired someone to start raking yet, or that someone had had the audacity to buy a mailbox that wasn't identical to everyone else's.

How many times had Joe woken to find tire tracks across his front yard? This is what rich teenagers did. They'd had everything handed to them, so deviance was the only thing they could give themselves. Three times in one year Joe had valuables stolen from his garage. The police always found them smashed and abandoned in the same ditch. "Probably just bored kids," they'd say, shrugging.

A year after Hanna died from brain cancer, Joe started paying attention to television advertisements for a nearby Neighborhood project. If he was going to raise a child on his own, he felt he at least needed the help of a good neighborhood. A real neighborhood.

He lit another cigarette. A few neighbors were talking and laughing on Mike Frederick's front porch. Joe smiled.

A Neighborhood realtor had explained to him that the idea of the Neighborhood was based loosely on the idea of the Victorian home in the Nineteenth Century. For the Victorian man, the home was a sanctuary, a place of peace and tranquility after dealing with the world's harsh realities. The man came home to a haven. "Of course, the Neighborhood isn't in any way chauvinist," the realtor assured him. "We have single mothers, working women, even a few low-key lesbians. And, we have single fathers like yourself. We take anyone who can subscribe to the idea of the perfect neighborhood and act accordingly." She explained that the Neighborhood offered the same sanctuary as the Victorian home, but owners didn't have to feel confined to their walls. "Once you drive through the gates, you are home. The people living around you truly are your neighbors. They know your name, offer to help you, lend you tools, invite you to barbecues—and not as though it's mandated. The people who choose to live here, live here because it provides a reality for what they always dreamed a neighborhood could be."

She explained that the Neighborhood offered homes in a wide range of prices. "This isn't like the area you're living in now. We don't exclude anyone based solely on wealth. Many people here are spending nearly every penny they have just to live in such an environment but, taking your income into account, money shouldn't be an issue. You might even consider one of our Everest models."

The Neighborhood made raising Stevie easier. He could go anywhere. He was always safe, always surrounded by positive influences. It was the kind of childhood Hanna had dreamed of for him. Joe was glad to be able to give it to him—even if it had to be as a widower.

A column of light filled his driveway, startling his fingertips and cheeks into tingling. He planted his cigarette into the soil and stood at the same time that the light went black and the engine went dead.

"Hello?" Joe called.

Footsteps scraped over the asphalt. Soon, a silhouette stood in the backyard.

Joe stepped forward away from what he was sure was a noxious cloud of smoke. "Who is it?"

"Is that you, Joe? It's me, Bill."

Joe took another few steps forward until Bill's face faded in through the darkness.

Bill looked over his shoulder toward the friendly voices gathered on Mike Frederick's porch. He turned back toward Joe. "What are you doing back here?"

"Smoking a cigarette" was the answer that came into Joe's head, but he managed to extinguish it. "I thought I heard a cat back here."

Bill nodded. "Maybe the Huston's cat?"

"Maybe." Joe shrugged.

"Smoky?"

Joe nearly swallowed his tongue. "Hmm?"

"Isn't their cat's name Smoky? No? Never mind." Bill apologized for stopping by unexpected. "So," he said, "what did you want to say about the proviso?"

Joe looked down. "Nothing, really. It can wait."

"Sure it can. As the Whip, though, I guess I would just like a heads-up. I really deserve to know before we all hear about it in front of Montgomery next month."

Joe pinched his eyes closed and rubbed his forehead. "I don't know, Bill. It's just that the whole thing seems a little dated, now. I mean, Willowbrook has a fire station only two miles from the gate. It just seems a strange regulation—"

"Are you saying you don't like living here?"

"What? Christ, Bill..." He caught himself. "Sorry."

Bill's face seemed to register the making of a mental note.

"It's just—"

"Joe. What we have here works because we have certain values. If we fling the gates open—"

"I'm not talking about flinging the gates. I'm just saying—"

"You're just saying what? That you want to let outsiders in? It's okay because it's just the fire department?" He shook his head. "Think, Joe. They don't just come to fight fires. They come to give our kids fire safety lessons in school. They come to do routine fire safety inspections on our buildings. They come to inspect hydrants. If we have no fire department, then they can come whenever they please. Is that what you want? Because I love this place too much to let that happen."

Joe stood slack-jawed. "I love it, too."

"Do you?"

"Yes."

Bill crossed his arms. "No outsiders, Joe. Period. What we have here falls apart otherwise."

Joe listened to the congenial sounds coming from Mike Frederick's porch. "Maybe you're right," he said.

The next month he retracted his request to discuss the proviso. Stone Montgomery smiled. "A little time to reflect can make anything look different," he said. Joe came home to several anonymous emails that asked why he had backed down. He deleted each without responding. In the months that followed, he said nothing at the meetings, listening only for Stevie's voice in that watery world.

Early November, Joyce Essinger and her husband invited Joe and everyone else on the block to a cocktail party. Mike Fredericks played the piano. Alyssa Cole and her husband sang. Joe stood at the large picture window and looked out at the emaciated silhouettes of bare trees. Hanna used to like to sing. He missed her.

Joyce touched his arm. "You've lost weight," she said. She seemed to study him when he turned toward her. "You don't look good. Have you been sleeping?"

He shrugged. "You know, lots to think about."

She nodded.

Her eyes looked like his had lately in the mirror—bloodshot, heavy, and hollow. The recent news had to have been on everyone's mind, though others in the room didn't look as haggard.

Within the last month, some outsiders had started tossing Molotov Cocktails over the walls of the two Los Angeles Neighborhoods. A Fire Sentinel had been severely disfigured and maimed in the line of duty. OptimiCorp assured residents that she was receiving the best treatment possible.

On one news talk program, an expert hypothesized that the assailants weren't angry at the residents themselves. OptimiCorp had been tied to several more water-related environmental scandals. "It flies in the face of the 2020 Water Shortage Act," the expert said. Neighborhoods were the company's most successful products. "Hit them where it hurts, I guess," the expert concluded.

"Follow me," Joyce said. She walked through the living room, the dining room, and then the kitchen. Looking over her shoulder first, she opened the basement door and started down into the darkness. Joe followed. The smells coming to him were damp and musty. He groped for the banister and then descended slowly, letting his feet find each step.

"I'm not going to turn on a light," Joyce said in the blackness at the bottom. "I'm sure you realize that our being gathered down here like this would be considered a breach of contract." She paused. "Basements are for spiders, not people," she said, quoting a popular Neighborhood slogan.

Mike's piano playing and the Coles' singing came faintly through the floor.

"Being gathered?" Joe asked.

Joyce explained that there were others in the basement. She asked them to say hello, and they whispered a greeting in unison. "As you can imagine," she said, "none of us can stay here for long. We want to get right to the point."

How many had he heard? Twenty? Thirty?

"We know that you had wanted to start a discussion on the Fire Sentinel proviso. We also know that you withdrew it." She was quiet for a moment. "We want you to raise the issue again."

Joe stood for a moment in the darkness, trying to let things sink in. "I don't ... I mean, why don't you raise the issue yourselves ... as a group?"

"We don't want to look like reactionaries. You already have a history with the issue. It would only make sense for you to bring it up again. Plus," Joyce said, "we think that Montgomery respects you ... that he would listen to you."

"If you do it," an unfamiliar male voice announced, "and it comes forward as a petition, we would support you. You wouldn't be alone."

It struck Joe that not everybody in the basement was necessarily from his Neighborhood. "Do you really think that Montgomery might listen to me?"

"We do," Joyce said. "That's why we're here."

"It was something you believed in for the community earlier," a new voice said. "We're just asking for you to believe in it again."

Joe thought of Stevie. Fifteen. Less than a year from his obligation. Maybe OptimiCorp would settle things by then. Or, maybe they would be much worse. The people gathered here believed that there was a chance. They believed Montgomery and the board might listen. Times were different. Maybe they would listen.

"I'll do it," Joe said.

A hand touched his upper arm and then moved to his shoulder. "Thank you," Joyce said. She squeezed. "We should get back up to the party."

Cold metal pressed against each of his hands.

"What are these?" he asked, trying to find a grip.

"Folding chairs," she said. "That's why we came down here."

December. Joe sat in the community center conference room waiting for Montgomery. He thought of his cigarettes. He'd been smoking nearly half a pack a day in his car to and from work. A cold rain blew against the window and slithered down the glass in wormy lines. He squeezed his coffee mug and heard it register a slight internal crack.

At the November meeting, Bill Anderson had tried to adjourn early, speaking of the packing he and Helen still needed to do before taking a four-day trip out of the Neighborhood for Thanksgiving.

"I would like to bring up some old business," Joe had said.

The others looked at him and then at Montgomery. It struck Joe that some who were sitting at the conference table might also have been in the darkness of Joyce's basement.

"What old business?" Bill asked, in a tone he usually reserved for Zach Watson.

Joe picked his hand up from the table. "It's regarding the Fire Sentinel proviso," he said, mopping at the moist impression of his palm with his sleeve.

Bill stared into Joe's eyes. "That's not old business. You retracted it. Since it never reached discussion, it's not—"

"It's okay, Bill."

Everyone turned toward Montgomery's looming face.

"I was planning to come there next month, anyway. If it's okay with everyone, I'll use our regular meeting time in December to discuss this one-on-one with Joe."

Joe wasn't sure what to think. Maybe Montgomery did respect him. Maybe he wanted to hear his thoughts.

Bill called Joe that night. "I'm the Whip. This should have come to me first." He said the whole thing made him look bad in front of Montgomery.

Joe switched the phone to his other ear. "I'm not trying to make you look bad. I'm just—"

"The Watsons are gone."

"What?"

"Zach Watson," Bill said. "The board exercised the right to buy his property back. Most of his recent behavior has amounted to spying on his neighbors. Extremely unneighborly, the board decided."

Joe's fingertips went cold. It occurred to him that Zach hadn't been at that night's meeting.

"The company gave Watson what he paid for the place. In two days they sold it for fifty thousand more to new buyers. People want in here, Joe. That's something to think about."

A long limousine pulled up to the community center, pulling Joe from his recollections. The driver emerged, opened an umbrella, and then went to the back door and opened it. Montgomery stepped out and under the umbrella. In a watery blur, the two figures moved up the sidewalk.

Joe drew in a long breath. He smoothed his hand over the three-page treatise he'd prepared. It explained why dropping the proviso was the best thing for the community.

Montgomery came into the conference room and shook the sleeves of his camel's hair coat. He was as tall as Joe had guessed, but not nearly as athletic. A huge turtle shell of a belly pressed against his white dress shirt. His face was paunchy and tinted pink, flaws the video equipment must have softened. He smelled of rain and cigars.

"Nasty out there," he said, giving his sleeves one last shake. He sat at the head of the table several seats from Joe. He unbuttoned but did not remove his coat.

"It's the time of year," Joe offered, wishing right after that he'd said nothing.

Montgomery studied him for a moment. His mouth rose into what seemed like an obligatory smile. "So, what is this all about regarding the proviso?"

Joe scratched the back of his neck and up into his hairline. "I've just been thinking that maybe it's time—"

"You do understand that living in the Neighborhood is not conscripted."

Joe's cheeks cooled as the blood rushed from them. "Stone?"

"Just restating the nature of the contract, Joe. If you're unhappy—"

"It's not that I'm un—"

Montgomery held up a finger to silence him. "I was going to say that if you're unhappy, the contract makes it easy to end services ... for either party."

Joe rubbed his fingertips over his eyelids. "It's not that I'm unhappy. Not at all. It's just that I think—"

Montgomery exhaled. "You know what the company is going through right now, don't you? You have to know that this is not the time for internal unrest."

"I know, but—"

"We're being attacked already. We can't be attacked from within, too. We can't afford to allow a fifth column."

"A fifth column?" Joe swallowed, sinking into his seat. The conversation seemed out of his hands.

Montgomery smiled after a moment. "I understand if that sounds dramatic, but I'm sure you can understand the pressure I'm under right now. We can't have any subversive activity that would undermine our best product."

Joe looked at the document he'd written.

Montgomery leaned back into his chair and set his big hands on the table. "If it makes any difference, the board has been discussing the proviso. They approved an amendment which would allow families to pay an override tax in lieu of service."

"An override tax?"

"Yes." Montgomery brushed a hand down his coat sleeve. "Of course, we are still working out the details. A new option on the product, if you will."

Stevie's voice rose clearly above the others in the pool room. "Check this out! Watch!" Joe pictured him on the diving platform shouting down to his friends bobbing in the water. His precious boy.

"How soon would it be available as an option?"

Montgomery stood. "A few months into the new year." He smiled again. "It won't be a cheap option, but an option."

Joe nodded.

Montgomery began to button his coat around his big belly. "What did you want to say, anyway?" He pointed at the pages. "It looks like you've prepared a statement."

Joe looked at the paper. "No. No, that's nothing." What of the faceless gathering in Joyce's basement? They couldn't even turn on a light. Let them fight their own battles.

"Good." Montgomery smiled. He put his hand on the doorknob. "If you can, stop by Bill's later for a drink."

Joe nodded. The rain came harder against the window. "Hey, Stone?" he called to the closing door.

Montgomery looked back into the room.

"Do you have kids?"

Montgomery smiled. "I have three."

Joe nodded. "They're great, aren't they? Kids, I mean."

"They are my prime movers," Montgomery said.

"Yeah."

"Merry Christmas, Joe."

The taillights on Montgomery's limousine flashed red, and then the car turned out of the parking lot. Joe put his hands on the pages in front of him. He'd used the words "we" and "our children." He'd used the phrase "the only right thing to do."

He leaned back into his seat. At least Stevie wouldn't have to be a Fire Sentinel. His service would be overridden. Joe made more money on the outside than he could ever hope to spend.

He imagined sneaking a final cigarette in the backyard later that evening—a celebration. His mouth watered. Listening for it, he could hear it almost every time he tried—Stevie's voice rising clearly over the cacophony of the others.

Lilac in October

The giant aromafiers filled the neighborhood with the heady scent of lilac. Sam Lincoln stood in his garage. His wife had mentioned that the week before the smell had been of apple pies baking. It was the first time since he'd moved his family into the new house that he was home on a weekend. Many of his sales calls took place on Saturdays, and it was easier to stay over until Monday, rather than fly home to turn around a day later and fly back.

A Vespucci Subdivision Security Vehicle crept past, the driver's head turning back and forth like a lawn sprinkler. Making eye contact with Sam, the officer smiled and lifted his hand.

Sam waved.

He thought of his sales numbers for September. He was up fourteen percent over the year before. Some of his colleagues were struggling. Sam once mentioned to the sales director that he could offer a workshop on his technique. The sales director just smiled in a way that wasn't really a smile. "Just keep doing whatever it is you're doing," he said. "Let the others sink or swim on their own."

A soothing sonata began. Sam checked his watch. Nine o'clock. He looked at the speakers mounted to the utility poles all along the street. In the evening he enjoyed the simulated sounds of the ocean that played until dawn, but the pumped-in classical music that rose and fell in volume throughout the day ate at him. Julie, though, said that she enjoyed it, and that's what was important. She was in the house much more than him.

Julie had taken their son Randy that morning to see her parents. She had wanted Sam to come. He reminded her that he had work to do around the house. "We'll have a good day together tomorrow," he said.

"Oh, so Randy and I will get to watch you sleep?" A moment later she apologized. "I know you need to get some things done around here. We'll see you later tonight—maybe around nine."

Gathering his tools, he thought he heard someone yelling somewhere in the neighborhood. He stopped and listened. The sonata rose in volume and dominated all sounds, except for the drone of a few lawnmowers.

Sam hefted the extension ladder from its place on the garage wall and carried it into the backyard. Most of the flowers that had been thriving when they'd moved in were dead or withering on their stalks. The lawn was yellowing into its dormancy. This weekend would probably be his last chance to get to the windows before the snow came.

Reaching the top of the ladder, he set his hand on the window ledge and then jerked it back. A spider's elaborate web spread outward from a lower corner of the window. Narrowing his eyes, Sam could just make out the spider's shadowy form drawn back inside a funnel of tightly woven web.

What a good life. Good home, steady supply of food, and nothing to worry about but itself. Sure, like every home owner, it had to fix broken strands every couple of days or sweep away the unsightly corpses. Sam grinned at the anthropomorphism, imagining the spider with a tiny broom. "Sorry," he said, when he finally used the squeegee to twist the web up like spaghetti. Suddenly homeless, the spider scurried up the exterior of the house. Reflexively, Sam crushed it with the sponge, twisting his hand back and forth. He apologized again.

Some time later, before starting the last window, he heard shouting again. He listened. The Brahms coming from the backyard speaker boomed. Sam glanced to his right. Then he stared. From where he stood, he could see over the ten-foot fence that enclosed his backyard. On the other side, down among the tree trunks, stood a small house with a small yard. More like a camp or a shack, it had a well and an outhouse.

A man in scarecrow clothes came from behind the tiny building. Roofing shingles lay scattered all over the ground. He picked them up and set them in the wheelbarrow he was pushing. More than half of his roof was nothing but tar paper. The few warped shingles that were still in place were covered with moss.

Two men came through the trees toward the house. Their filthy clothes, ground in with dirt, looked to have been at one time some kind of uniform. Dark blue pants with gray stripes down the legs. Gray button-up shirts with dark blue stripes down the sleeves. Their time-worn black boots went up to their knees. The man with the wheelbarrow spotted them and held his arms out to block them. Their faces and mouths moved with shouting. Heart racing, Sam heard nothing over the oboes, flutes, violins and glockenspiel.

The men shoved the lone man. He pushed back. They overpowered him, and he fell backwards, ramming a kidney against the wooden handle of the wheelbarrow. He writhed on the ground, and the other men upended his load and kicked the shingles over the ground again. Before leaving, they turned their kicking on him. He held his hands over his face, taking the blows to his forearms and stomach.

The violence left Sam frozen and nauseated with adrenaline. The two men turned and left. Watching them disappear into the trees, Sam spotted a second building. Three young men sat on the ground in front of the dilapidated shack. Each grimaced, holding his abdomen. A small fire smoldered in a pit near their feet. One of them rose quickly and stumble-jogged over to a thin tree. He pulled down his pants. Squatting, he held the tree with one hand, planted his feet by its base, and leaned back like a water skier. He suspended his rear end as far out as he could. A watery discharge of diarrhea gushed from him onto the leaves.

Sam turned away and started down the ladder. His heart seemed to want out of his ribcage.

"I'll be up on a ladder myself, today."

Sam's heart jumped in its racing, and he clutched the rungs to keep his balance. A blonde man in a polo shirt and jeans was at the bottom of the ladder holding it steady with his left hand. "Didn't mean to startle you," he said.

"It's okay," Sam said, finishing his descent.

"My wife wants me to put our new shutters up," the man said, extending his hand to Sam when he reached the ground. "I'm your neighbor from across the street. Harold Brown." He smiled. "Just Hal," he said.

Sam said his own name and shook Hal's hand. The smell of lilac was thick around them.

"Looks like you're away from home as much as I am. In the last month..." Hal studied Sam. "You okay?"

Sam blinked and looked at him. He pointed toward the trees. "There are houses in there. People."

Hal looked toward the fence and shook his head. "You didn't know about them?"

Sam stared. "Know about them? How could I—"

"Look, nothing ever happens," Hal said. "I've been here four years. There's never been a problem. Most of the time you won't even—"

"That's easy for you to say. They're right next to my house."

Hal scratched his upper lip. "The sub is full of them. Probably more places like that than there are places like ours."

Sam couldn't take his eyes from the trees. A thin wisp of smoke rose above the fence. He smelled only lilac.

"I'm telling you, though, don't worry about them. Nothing's ever happened."

"I just saw something happen."

"Yeah, well, nothing's ever happened over here."

"Nothing?"

Hal shrugged. "Two years ago one of them killed himself by setting his place on fire. Security got hoses to the trees so fast that we didn't even lose one. Just some damage to some of the branches. They had the fence back up that same evening."

Sam remembered his tour through a burn unit. "That's a helluva way to go," he said. It'd been nearly ten years since he'd dropped out of med school to take a position as a medical technology sales rep.

Hal waved his hand at the fence dismissively. "They're all crazy. They bring it on themselves. The guy behind me? His place looks ready to fall over. I told him through the fence once that he should get someone to raise his house and have the foundation rebuilt. You know what he said?"

Sam shrugged.

"He said, 'Easy for the goldfinch to tell the rabbit to simply fly away when the fox is near.'" Hal laughed. "I'm telling you ... crazy."

Sam pointed. "I don't think it's funny. The men over there were fighting. One man looked pretty hurt."

Hal shook his head.

Sam pointed at the cell phone on his belt. "I thought of calling security."

"They wouldn't have done anything."

Sam looked at him.

"The security isn't for them," Hal said.

Sam looked toward the fence again. He couldn't see anything through the shadow box design.

"Look, I just thought I should introduce myself. Be neighborly," Hal said, smiling. "Now, I have to get to those shutters." He held out his hand again.

Sam shook it. "Okay. Thanks for stopping."

"Hey, let's get our families together the next time you and I are both home." Hal chuckled. "When do you think that will be? In about a year?" Laughing, he walked around the corner of the house and disappeared.

Sam paced the backyard. A violin concerto began. Climbing the ladder to retrieve his equipment from the window ledge, he looked over the fence. The man lay on the ground next to his overturned wheelbarrow. His eyes were closed. Sam took a few breaths and tried to call to him. The music drowned out his efforts. He looked at the other house and its fire pit. Smoke rose in nearly invisible wisps. The young men were gone.

He used his ladder to climb to the other side of the fence. The man stirred when Sam rolled him onto his back. An odor of sweat rose from his body. His mouth hung open. His yellow front teeth faded back into black molars.

"Are you okay?" Sam asked.

Squinting at him for a moment, the other man opened his eyes fully. He scrambled away, but went only a few feet before he stopped and gripped his stomach.

"I'm not going to hurt you. I saw what those other men did."

The pain slowly left the man's face.

"Are you okay?"

The man nodded. "I must have passed out." He studied Sam's clothes.

"I thought maybe you were ... the way you were lying here. You looked really bad."

The other man stared.

Sam smiled. "I want to help." He crouched over him, gripped the other man under his arms, waited a moment to make sure he understood, and then raised him to his feet.

The man steadied himself against the side of the house.

Sam righted the wheelbarrow and bent for a few shingles. "What happened to your roof?"

The man looked up toward his eaves. "The winds last week took most of it off."

Sam remembered that Julie had told him over the phone about a bad thunderstorm that had blown through. Their home had seen no damage.

The shingles felt brittle. Sam set them gingerly into the wheelbarrow. He bent for more. "Who were those men?"

"My brothers."

Sam looked at him. "Why would they do that to you?"

The man shrugged. "They're trying to break me." He pointed. "They want me to run away from my house so they can take it for themselves."

Sam looked at the tumbledown little house. He made a face that must have been asking a question.

"The well has good water," the man said.

Sam helped with the rest of the shingles. Odors came to him as he worked. Smoke. The earthy smell of fallen leaves. Wafts of the other man's body on the air. Sometimes his own odor came up to him, rising through the mask of his deodorant.

He heard noises in the woods. Quarreling. The low moans of chronic pains. Children trying to play. There was a life here he knew nothing about. The music of his own yard sounded far away. He worked intently, bending for the shingles. He was on the other side of the tiny house when the rhythm of steady footsteps came across the leaf-strewn ground.

"Up again so soon?" a man's voice said.

Sam walked around the corner. The man had his arms spread out, trying to block his brothers from the wheelbarrow. "No," he said. They lunged at him and again threw him to the ground.

"Stop it," Sam shouted. His heart ran with fear like a rabbit. He took a step forward.

The other men, in their threadbare, filthy uniforms, stepped back.

Sam took in their paling faces. He was taller than both of them. He pointed. "Just go home," he said. He helped the other man back to his feet. "Leave him alone."

"Who the hell are you all of a sudden?"

Sam stepped forward again and moved them back another pace. "Just walk away." He swept his hands across the air in front of him. "Don't come back here again."

They stared. "This has nothing to do with you."

"Just go."

The men looked at each other, communicated something in their silence, and then started to retreat through the trees. The bigger of the two turned. "This isn't over," he said, not looking at Sam, but at the other man.

"It needs to be over," the man said.

"It's over," Sam said.

When his brothers were gone, the man thanked Sam. Wanting to do more, Sam went back over the fence. He drove to a hardware store and bought plywood, bitchethane, and new shingles for the small roof. Using rope, he hauled them up to the top of the fence and lowered them down to the other side. He brought tools over with him. It was nearly dark by the time they had the old shingles and tar paper off. They had stripped the roof down to bare rafters.

"Doesn't look like rain tonight," Sam said, looking up into the dusk's dim stars. "You should be okay until tomorrow."

The other man took Sam's hand in both of his. "You are like someone out of the Bible." He bent and braided his fingers into a step. Sam put his foot in the other man's hands and let himself, at the count of three, be hoisted to the top of the fence. Before disappearing into his own yard, Sam told the man that he would be back.

Julie and Randy weren't home. Sam ate and then lay on the couch to wait for them.

An absence of light and sound woke him. He opened his eyes. Julie was standing by the television.

"How are your parents?" he asked, sleepily.

She turned. "I didn't mean to wake you up. I can put it back on."

He said it was okay. "Where's Randy?"

"I put him to bed when we got home. He was exhausted." She sat down in the chair across from the couch.

They talked for a moment about her parents, who were planning a trip to Cozumel.

"Do you know about the woods?" Sam then asked, not knowing how she would react.

"The woods?"

He sat up on the couch. "In the trees just beyond our fence. There are houses back there ... people living in them."

Her face changed and she nodded. "Yes, I know." She looked toward the picture window blackened with night.

"You never told me," he said.

"I meant to, but I had to wait to talk with you, and then it was over the phone. There were other things. I'd forgotten," she said.

"You forgot?"

She shrugged. "I don't think about them."

Sam muttered.

"What?" she asked.

"Nothing."

"No, what, Sam? Do you think you have something to say?"

He rubbed a hand over his face. "I just don't see ... I mean, how can you not think about them? They're right—"

Julie laughed hollowly. "How can I not think about them? Jesus, Sam, I don't know—maybe because I'm a married woman raising a child like a single mother."

He looked at her. Her neck was flushed red up to her ears.

"It's just me here," she said, pointing at herself. "Alone. I help him with his homework. I wake up with him at two in the morning when he's sick. I talk to him when he's having

150

problems ... it's not fair of you to sit here and tell me what I should and shouldn't be thinking about." She stood and started for the kitchen. "I've got plenty to think about when you're gone all the time."

He cleared his throat. "I went over the fence."

She stopped and turned. "What?"

He told her about that afternoon and what he'd done.

She stood for a moment, looking dazed. She shook her head. "They could have really hurt you, even..."

"Well, they didn't." He stood up. "They were more scared than—"

"You don't know what they might have done. You don't know."

He sat again. "Nothing bad happened, Julie. It just felt really ... I haven't felt that way in a long time."

She pointed at him. "You have to..." She pulled her finger back and made a small fist. She squeezed it. "You just can't take risks like that." She turned to walk out of the room. "Jesus, Sam, they might have even killed you."

"I want to do more."

She stopped.

"You forget..." he started, "you forget how powerful you can be. One person. But you forget. I mean, you really feel like you can't do anything most of the time ... like we're all so small." He ran his fingers through his hair. "This ... what I was doing. It just felt big. And, the money—it was so little to us. Cost us nothing, really."

She came into the room and sat on the couch next to him. "Sam." She waited until he looked at her. "I know what you ... but you can't ... you just have to be careful. It might have cost us everything." She squeezed his thigh. "Where are we without you? What happens to us if something happens to you?"

"If I do more, it wouldn't have to be dangerous." He rubbed his eyes. "I mean, even if I volunteered in a soup kitchen ... some kind of charity—"

"Charity?" She gave a sympathetic chuckle. "You have a charity right here in this house."

He looked at her.

"Your son? If you have all of this extra time, give it to him. Wrestle with him. Take him fishing. Talk to him." She took his hand in hers and squeezed. "He never sees you."

The word "never" resonated in his head.

She stood and started to leave the room again. "When was the last time you spent any time with him?" She turned. "You could do something pretty big right here in this house."

As though the sounds of the ocean just outside his window were from a real body of water, he felt blindsided by a huge wave—left limp in the surf.

He climbed the stairs and looked in on his boy. The back of his small head lay on the pillow. The blankets moved slightly with his breathing. Sam crawled in with him, and Randy's thin body turned instinctively to the warmth. His delicate hand settled on Sam's chest. His legs drew up and wrapped around his thigh. Sam felt his own warmth against the thin, cool legs. Seven years old. So little muscle, really. The boy was chilled. It wouldn't be many more days before they'd have to start using the furnace. He would need to get it inspected.

He pet his son's hair. Asleep as it was his little face seemed so vulnerable. Julie was right.

Lying with Randy, Sam thought of his own youth. It was an image from twenty-five years before in a bus depot. His father stood with his hand gripped over a smearing of blood. His suture site was bleeding, wicking up through his sweatshirt. Two days earlier he'd had his appendix out. He'd heard from one of Sam's friends that Sam was planning to take off for Andover, Kansas to volunteer to help with post-tornado efforts. The place had been declared a disaster area. Sam was only seventeen. Even post-operative, his father had been enough of a father to show up to stop him. Looking at his bleeding father, Sam had given no argument. He canceled his ticket and went home.

Nearly asleep, he imagined noises coming from beyond the fence—the sounds of trespassing, vandalism, theft, assault.

He went to the fence and climbed over. He drove the men away again and then kept watch until the morning. He helped nail the shingles down in rows. Julie and Randy called faintly to him over the fence, over the music. They screamed and, when he finally looked, his own house was on fire.

He opened his eyes and rubbed his hands over his face. He took a long breath.

A dream. Just a dream.

A storm brewed wildly over the ocean. Randy shivered. Sam drew the blankets tighter around himself and his son, a funnel of warmth. The waves crashed on the shore. He tried to convince himself that he would go over the fence again sometime. I have to, he thought. Sinking through the layers of coming sleep, he was soothed by the fragrance of lilac all around them.

Following a Stupid Man

I've been following a stupid man for two days. A stupid man with money. I follow him because I know he will need me—need my words. He has come to México although he does not know the language. He has come because he has heard that his dollar will go a long way. His friends have told him about the deals. And they've told him things about las mujeres, the women. He has not come because he knows something about the land or the people. For him, this country is a cheap hotel, a pawnshop. A bordello. Stupid as he is though, I follow him. He gives me coins when I talk for him—American coins. American coins sound different in the hand than Mexican coins. Mexican coins sound thin and high-pitched. American coins sound fat.

"Tell him I want that spoon," estúpido tells me to tell the shopkeeper. A small spoon hangs between two small nails on the wall behind the counter.

The owner follows us around his small shop. He is old and he walks as though his legs are wearing out. Anyone can see he has basura in his shop—garbage. Estúpido must know it. I think even the shopkeeper knows it, but what he has he has, so he follows us, hoping that estúpido is stupid enough.

The shopkeeper glares at me as though he would hit me. "I have some American words," he says.

"Don't bother, I'll use the kid," estúpido says. He turns to me. "Tell him I want that spoon."

The shopkeeper follows the pointing finger and starts to shake his head before I can translate. "La cuchara era de mi madre y de su madre antes y de su madre antes de esto." He explains that the small spoon was his mother's and her mother's before that and before that her mother's.

"No sell," the shopkeeper says.

Estúpido looks at me. "What?" he asks.

I tell him what the shopkeeper said.

"For Chrissakes. Tell him I'll give him ten bucks."

Ten dollars American is a lot of money—a day's worth of profits for the shopkeeper, maybe more. The americano must know something about small spoons. He must know where he can get fifty for it. And for me, after we are through, he will have nickels, dimes.

I turn to tell the shopkeeper, but he knows enough American. He's already shaking his head.

"Oh, come on," the americano says, "Ten dollars is a great deal for you. The spoon's a gift for a woman back home. My boss' wife. She collects the goddamned things."

The shopkeeper shrugs and then shakes his head.

The store is quiet then. I hear many voices in the street shouting what there is to sell, how fair their prices, how valuable their wares. They speak loudly and slowly so the gringos can understand them.

"Twenty bucks," estúpido says.

"No sell."

I look at the spoon. It is smaller than my hand, held in place only by the two nails that cradle it. It would be easy to steal.

Estúpido shakes his head. "Will you tell him he's got nothing but dog shit in this shop. You've got NOTHING, NADA," he shouts into the face of the shopkeeper. "This is exactly why your country is so poor. This was the deal of a lifetime for you, Pedro. Twenty bucks for a spoon and he says no. Jesus Christ."

Estúpido walks out. I don't tell the shopkeeper anything but he has enough American to know he has been insulted. I imagine he's counting the ways he could have used the twenty dollars. He glances sheepishly around his shop. Then he looks at the spoon and crosses himself. When he looks at me again he speaks in Spanish. "You get out you little bastard."

I catch up to estúpido. The way he carries himself reminds me of my uncle's words. "Most have been American too long," I've heard him say. "For them, with their money, the rest of the world is a circus. They don't see that everywhere is human bones and blood."

Sometimes I go listen to my uncle at the barra across the street from where he works. I like the pictures in his sentences. He sits with other men from work and they listen to him until he gets too drunk. My uncle and the other men work in the General Motors automobile factory. They say the factory at one time had been in some American town. They don't seem to mind that I sit and listen.

My uncle speaks of a unión and the need to organize. He talks about benefits, job security, and workplace safety. This part of his talk bores me. But if he talks and drinks for long enough, his Spanish will flair with color and volume.

"If the trabajadores americanos were stupid because they asked for too much, aren't we just as stupid for taking too little? Running from one end of a burning ship to the other will not save you—it just means you die slower. I do not want to be a scurrying rat down in the hold, blind, not realizing that the whole ship is going down anyway."

Many of the men stare down into their drinks at this point, but I listen to my uncle closely. This is why I've come—to see his words.

"Is that what any of you want? To be rats cowering from the gringo fat cats? Do you want to feel your joints slowly become hinges? Do you want to feel those hinges slowly rust? The factory will not oil those hinges for you. Once you rust they get rid of you and replace you with new machines. If we stay as we are without fighting then we become machines. I will not become a slave to their money," my uncle will say, slamming the table with his fist after each statement. "I am a man!"

The other men slowly get up and leave my uncle. Maybe they are waiting for the day he will drink little enough that he will actually rise and start his unión. Maybe they are just tired of his talk—tired of the pictures in his words. The pictures are always sad.

When he notices the men are gone, my uncle stops drinking beer and orders tequila. He tells me to shut up when I ask him questions. His flaming words are then done, but sometimes they come back to me. Sometimes when I think of them they make me say things I would do better not to say.

"That spoon was in his family a long time," I say to the americano as I follow him. "Here that's important."

He screws up his face. "What?"

"He needs that spoon to remember," I say.

"Remember what?" he asks.

His madre, I think. Here we remember our mothers—honor them. I think of my own mother any time I see a long braid of black hair. When I was smaller I often sat on the stool behind my mother in the kitchen. Her back was to me because she was always cooking. She cooked for us, she cooked for others in the neighborhood, and she cooked for the men who stopped by our home. Her favorite were enchiladas. I can smell them as I think of them. Enchiladas de queso, enchiladas de pollo, enchiladas verdes, suizas, tapatias ... and she loved making mole poblano, though many of the men who came by would not eat it. "Tan rico y misterioso como México si mismo," she would say—as dark and mysterious as Mexico itself. Her long braid swept her wide buttocks as she moved between stove and counter. She told me that many men liked her hair that long.

While I would sit with her, my mother would tell me stories from the Biblia. And she would tell me the meaning of each. She told me that her madre had told the same stories. Many of the stories were of men so taken up in the world that they often overlooked God. One story she often told was of a Samaritan. She said this story was the most important because it showed us the one way we could all make the world better. Another story she often told was of Jesús and a prostitute, but she never explained the meaning.

I do not have many memories of my mother. She died of VIH, perder enfermedad, when I was only seven. And my father I never knew. So I hold onto the memories of my mother that I do have.

I imagine the shopkeeper needs to remember his madre too. He looks at the spoon and remembers her and her poorness and the long line of poorness that came before her.

And being that poor all she had were words, and she told him that even when you're poor you have to give. She told him that there were poorer people—people who were dying their minutes instead of living them. She told him to help them. It's the only way to be rich.

And maybe when nobody was around and it was dark, his mother needed the spoon too to remember, and her mother before her. That spoon may have been at the Last Supper—some camarera, eavesdropping on it all, took the spoon to remember, kept it in her family, started passing on the words. They are the words my mother told me when she was alive.

"Never mind, don't explain it," the americano says. "And stop following me." He throws me a quarter, turns, and walks away.

An hour later I find him. I follow him at a distance. Then I see him trying to talk with a man I've seen on the streets before. The americano flips his hands and shakes his head. He looks cheerless, tired. I walk up and see the other man has a towel full of cheap switchblades. They look down at me.

"Oh," the americano says, "it's you. Tell him I'll give him twenty bucks for that one."

I look in the towel and then back at the americano. "You don't want these. Junk. The insides are no good." I have seen blades like these before. They spring a few times and then stop.

The americano looks at me for a few seconds. Then he puts his hand over the towel and waves it back and forth. "No," he says and walks away.

I follow him. I can hear the man with the blades behind me hissing threats in Spanish. He will remember me. I will need to watch out for him.

The americano walks a few blocks. Then he stops. "Do you know where I can get a decent switchblade?"

I think and then shake my head.

The americano exhales and walks another block. Then he stops again. "I thought I told you to STOP following me."

I wish I could stop following him. I reach into my pocket, bring the spoon out, and hold it up to his face.

"How'd you get it?" he asks, smiling.

I don't say anything. He reaches out and takes the spoon. He holds it for a moment, but his face looks as though he is thinking about something else. His smile turns straight. Soon he starts turning the spoon over. Then he runs his thumbnail down the back of it. He shakes his head.

"This isn't what I thought it was," he says. "This isn't worth what I thought, kid."

He reaches into his pocket and takes out a handful of change. "The spoon is worth nothing to me," he says, "but I will give you this." He puts the change in my hand. Quarters, dimes, nickels, pennies—maybe two dollars. He puts the spoon in his shirt pocket. "Now get lost."

I think of the way the shopkeeper chased me when I took the spoon. I remember how he tripped. I can still hear the hollow sound his mouth made when he fell. I did not wait to see if he rose again.

The americano starts walking. I do not go after him. I wish I had never taken the spoon. He is disappearing into the crowded street, and I have trouble following him with my eyes. His head, though, is above everybody else's, and that helps me for some time. But I know that I will lose him. Part of me wants to let him vanish—to see the dark heads of Mejicanos consume his. Part of me wants the people to turn on him—to tear him to pieces. But a bigger part of me knows that somebody else will begin following him, begin translating for him. He will give money to somebody else. I want so badly to do anything other, but I run and catch up close enough that I can follow at a distance. He will need me again. Stupid men always need someone to translate.

It makes me sad sometimes to follow such men for their coins, but it's the only way I know. Who else do I have to follow? I've seen little so far that tells me my mother's words are true. And I know too that she was just a whore. My uncle often teases me and tells me that my father was probably an americano. He says it's why I learned American so quickly.

I can't follow my uncle either—not into the sweaty factory. I see how he has changed. I see how he is tired all the time. No deseo mi bisagra para aherrumbrar—I do not wish my hinge to rust. I respect my uncle's talk, but his words are simply a fiery way to describe the things that no one will ever be able to change.

No, I will follow the stupid man. I know the only things I can really believe in are the coins in my pocket. I rub them together. I will try to make them go a long way.